"Why should I surrender?" the war chief asked.

Horn said nothing.

"A Chiricahua can run seventy miles in a day. Can a whiteskin?"

"No," Horn answered. "But we have five thousand warriors and you have nineteen."

"When we attack, it is a massacre; when you attack, it is a battle. Is that just?" Geronimo thundered.

"No. But we have five thousand warriors and you have nineteen."

"You pay twenty dollars for the scalp of an Indian baby. And you call us cruel. And to such a people, you say I should surrender!"

"No," said Horn.

"You have said I should surrender," the great chief cried.

"I have said you *must* surrender," Horn replied.

MR. HORN

A novel by
D. R. BENSEN

*Adapted from the screenplay by
William Goldman*

A DELL BOOK

Published by
Dell Publishing Co., Inc.
1 Dag Hammarskjold Plaza
New York, New York 10017

Dell ® TM 681510, Dell Publishing Co., Inc.

ISBN: 0-440-15194-5

Printed in the United States of America
First printing—December 1978

CHAPTER 1

From where he hunkered on the huge boulder, he could see, far off, the arid hills closing in the horizon, red-brown in the noon sun, and, closer, the cattle grazing on the lush tall grass, closer yet, a dozen horses, patient and tethered, cropping at what forage they could reach.

The sharp edge of the rock cut off his view of the horses' owners, though he could hear their desultory talk drifting up from below. He didn't care to see them and he would just as soon they didn't see him.

He squinted across to the distant hills and then blotted them out with the glinting green of the whiskey bottle he held to his mouth.

Eleven men squatted, sat, knelt, or lay near the rickety chuck wagon, some positioning themselves so that their broad hat brims gave some shade from the sun, others accepting its glare and heat as the price of relaxing muscles tensed by hours in the saddle. The twelfth was the only one standing, enduring the heat from the chuck-wagon stove as well as that of the sun as he stirred with a long ladle in a blackened iron pot. The air above the pot shimmered and wavered, making the face of the giant boulder behind it seem liquid, like a rock transformed into a waterfall.

Four of the cowpunchers were playing poker without much interest. "See you an' raise you twenty," one said, shoving two wooden matches across the ground to join a heap of them that lay in the center of the group.

"Red-head matches is five, not ten," another player observed. "Blue-head is ten. You're just seein', not raisin', with that bet."

"Blues, five; reds, ten; that's the way it was set at the beginnin'," the first player protested.

"But that 'us before the whole pot caught fire two days back," the third man said, "an' left us withouten hardly any blue-heads amongst us, so they become the scarcest, whiles as it was the other way around before then. So natcherly the blues is the more valuable an' is now rated at ten dollars, an' the reds at five."

The first player shook his head. "Be simpler was we playin' for cash. No confusin' two bits with a double eagle, that's for certain."

The last man in the circle looked up from a glum examination of his cards. "On Valley Ranch pay, the question ain't about to arise. Was they to pay us in double eagles, a month's wages'd git lost in your pockets."

"You're forgettin' the 'and found' part of the deal," the third player said. "Cash wages, plus keep an' maybe some free saddlery repairin' thrown in. A man that don't go in for dissipations, such as enjoyin' himself, can bank pretty near four hundred a year, livin' like a king at the boss's expense the whole time." He rose, sauntered toward the chuck wagon, and called to the cook, "Beans done?"

The cook looked up from his stirring and nodded. "Wamme to tell him?" the cardplayer said, jerking his head toward the overhanging boulder.

"He can see," the cook said shortly. To his way of thinking, a man who would wander away from the area of the cookstove while lunch was being prepared was unnatural, and not showing appreciation of the hard, skilled work being done on his behalf. A *lot* of cooks wouldn't take the trouble to soak the beans long enough or to make sure there was always a piece of salt pork to drop in the pot.

The cowboy nodded and shrugged. The cook took a tin plate from a pile next to the stove, ladled a mound of beans onto it, and handed it to him. The clink of the ladle against the pot rim roused the other men from their occupations or lack of them, and they began drifting toward the chuck wagon.

The distant sound of the serving of the noon meal and the aroma of the beans did not seem to affect the solitary man on top of the rock. He set the whiskey bottle down beside him, rose, and went to where his horse stood head down as if close inspection of the rock might reveal something worth eating.

A coil of rope, secured by two dangling leather thongs tied together, hung from the saddle. The man undid these and held the rope in his hands. It was slick and supple, smooth and pliant as a snake, as if it had been lovingly tended and worked on for many hours.

With a flick of his wrist he snapped the coil open.

The rope settled to the ground about him in a wide loop, held in that shape by a noose so smoothly spliced that it seemed like a natural part of the rope. Another motion of the wrist sent the loop spinning around him, inches above the flat surface of the rock; lazily at first, then faster and faster.

"Rider," one of the feasting cowhands said, jerking his head toward the west.

The man next to him looked in the same direction. "New orders from the boss, d'you think?"

The first man shook his head. "Ain't Sharkey or any of them from the ranch, I c'n tell. Ain't nobody as I ever see."

In a few moments the rider, a burly, bearded man looking to be about fifty, came up to them. He leaned from the saddle to ask a question.

The man who had first spotted him gave him a curious look and gestured with his fork toward the overhanging rock. The rider nodded and moved off the grassland. His horse picked its way expertly over the rough surface, and in a few moments he was at the top, where he dismounted. A curious whipping sound drew him toward a large rock fragment, from behind which the noise was coming; he limped, favoring his right foot. He came around the boulder and stopped to watch in astonishment.

In the noon sun, the lean, whirling figure cast fluid, darting shadows which flowed on the rock like ink. The looped lariat spun around in a blur, as if it were alive, sinking almost to the ground, then rising to his chest. Without stopping or altering its motion, he leaped in and out of the spinning circle, partnering the rope in an intricate dance.

The man on horseback shook his head wonderingly. It was uncanny, a little *schrecklich*, this lone man driving himself to do something perfectly—something most men couldn't do and wouldn't want to. But that made it all the more certain that it was the man he was after.

Suddenly aware of the intruder, the rope wielder in an instant stopped his gyration; the lariat fell slackly to the rock. He turned his back on the horseman and began to walk away.

The rider called after him, "I seek Mr. Horn."

The man stopped and turned, his face an expressionless area of shadow under the hat brim.

"You are the Talking Boy?" the rider said.

The man nodded.

"My name is —"

"You're Sieber, aren't you?"

The rider was inwardly pleased. Being the chief civilian scout in the Arizona Territory was not a job that made one a famous public figure, but it was good to know that, after twenty years of it, someone at least recognized him. He felt more than ever sure that his man, strange as he was, was the one he wanted. "It is so." Sieber gestured out toward the grazing cattle. "You like this, working for the Valley Ranch?"

"Not so much this year as last year," Horn said flatly.

"Good," Sieber said. "You come work for me as assistant. Big opportunity, big salary; one dollar a day."

Horn considered the offer. Some better than a cow-

9

poke's pay, anyhow, he thought; and for sure, it'd be a change. "What would I do?"

"I'll tell you as we go, but now we must get to Fort Bowie."

"Long way," Horn said.

Sieber nodded, fished in his saddlebag, and held up an almost empty bottle of whiskey. "It's a three-quart ride." He gestured toward Horn's horse. "Come—we get to the ranch now and you pack. Whatever you own."

"Everything?" Horn asked.

Sieber nodded again. "How long will that take you?"

Horn looked out over the grasslands and listened for a moment to the sounds of his companions of the last two years finishing their meal. How long to finish off a stretch like that, close to a tenth of his whole life . . . to get together everything he had to show for twenty-some years . . . ?

He swung into his saddle and set his horse toward the rearward slope of the rock. "Ten minutes."

CHAPTER 2

"That's the choice, gentlemen," the storekeeper said. "Green River er Old Brigham, each the finest whiskey of its type available."

"Get the Old Brigham," Horn advised.

He and Sieber laid down the coins the storekeeper required of them and took possession of three bottles of whiskey each. Cradling these, they walked through the area of the small general store devoted to goods and sundries toward the outer door.

"The Old Brigham's some stronger?" Sieber asked. "Or cheaper?"

Horn shook his head. "Green River got a picture of cows an' scenery on the label," he said. "Old Brigham's got three women, one of 'em mighty good-looking, along with old Young an' his beard. Whiskey's the same, they make it out back of the store, but I druther have a handsome woman lookin' back at me while I'm takin' a drink than a wall-eyed cow."

He emphasized this statement of his preference by returning the nodded greeting of a well-set-up young woman behind the store counter. Sieber squinted at her and speculated about just how well his new aide might have come to know her over the past two years.

The store was the only establishment of its kind convenient to the Valley Ranch, and Horn would have had to have patronized it. Evidently it didn't bother him to be leaving; he hadn't troubled to tell her goodbye.

Outside the store, as they stowed the whiskey in their saddlebags, sliding each bottle into a sock to avoid the tragedy of breakage, Sieber asked Horn, "You like that girl?"

Horn shrugged. "All right. I like women my own age better."

Sieber shook his head. It must have been twenty years since the difference between twenty-five or -six—that would be how old Horn was, he guessed—and twenty, give or take a year on either side, which was how he pegged the girl, had seemed important to him. Anybody, man or woman, under thirty, thirty-five, was young—once you got to Sieber's age, no matter how you felt inside, you were old. "Too skinny," he said. "Listen to me now, I save you grief later. The best thing a woman can be is fat. Once they're fat, they don't expect nothing." He thought for a moment before passing on a further bit of wisdom. "Sad, too. Women that aren't sad aren't worth a shit."

Horn looked at him with muted amusement. "All you got to do is find yourself a fat unhappy lady and you're set for life."

Quite seriously, Sieber said, "I been lookin'," as he mounted his horse.

By later afternoon they were in arid, desolate country where only the most inept cattle would venture in search of grazing. The heat rose from sand and rock to cook Horn inside his clothes; but the air was so dry that almost all the sweat evaporated before it could make him feel clammy. He contemplated taking a swig of water from his canteen, but decided in favor of a pull at the first of his three quarts of whiskey. Didn't do much toward quenching thirst, but nothing short of a hogshead of water would do that, anyhow. The heat of the whiskey going down sort of fought the heat biting at him, he figured, and held it to a draw. Same principle as the chili the Texicans were so set on, he now saw, get hot enough on the inside and you don't mind how parched you are on the outside. Might work just the other way around in cold weather; suck on a piece of ice or such in the winter, and maybe you wouldn't mind the cold. Nobody'd ever thought of that yet, for sure, at least he'd never heard it recommended. Another advantage of the whiskey was that it opened up your mind to original thoughts like that, kept you feeling interested in things even on a goddam dumb long ride like this.

"Mr. Sieber?" he called.

The scout looked over toward him, one broad hand clutching his own whiskey bottle, a shade less full than Horn's. Horn gave an inward chuckle as he saw that Sieber's thumb was pressed squarely against the best-looking Mrs. Young's most interesting prospect.

"You really been shot twenty-eight times?"

Siever gave him a disgusted look. "Who told you that?"

"Just what you hear," Horn said.

Sieber shook his head. "People will say *anything*. Who could be shot twenty-eight times and live?"

Horn considered this. When you looked at it closely,

the statement had the earmarks of a tall tale, all right.

"I've been *wounded* twenty-eight times," Sieber said carefully. He drank from his bottle. "But some were knives, and some arrows, and at least a couple clubs." He laughed. "Twenty-eight times shot!" After another drink, he shook his head and said, "Ridiculous!"

A little farther along the way, he said, "Once is enough for most men."

"Once of what?" Horn asked.

"Getting shot."

"Bang," Horn said vaguely. He eyed the bottle he held and decided against another drink just now. He had the strong feeling that if his horse stumbled, or even if it didn't, that he might be hard put to it to keep in the saddle.

"I was lucky," Sieber said.

"When?"

"At Gettysburg. Ball went through my ankle, besmashed it to hellangone, that's why I walk funny."

Horn tried to sort out the luck involved in being left with a permanent limp, but Siever continued before he could frame a question. "That was *my* bullet. Most of the fellows I seen there, it was one shot done them. Like wheat in a field when the mowers been through, laying there, some you couldn't see where it hit them, some maybe a blue spot on the forehead, a hole in the coat. Others, back at the field hospitals, yelling while the surgeons took off a leg or arm or what, or just yelling and crying with a bullet where there wasn't nothing anybody could do about it. So just a bum ankle, a gimpy walk, from Gettysburg that was luck.

14

You know, there was more fellows killed in that fight, three days only, than in all this Indian business out here these last twenty years? Even counting pig-head Custer and them. And all through it, I never figured what it was about."

"How come you was in it, then?" Horn asked.

Sieber looked at him. "Them times, you was for or against, especially when you come from Europe and say, I want to be an American. Government says, Fine; we'll make an American out of you right away, all you got to do is shoot the ass off a bunch of other Americans that don't want to be Americans anymore."

Horn sighed. He'd been five when the war—The War—had ended, and remembered only that there'd been a lot of hoorawing about that, and about Lincoln getting killed just at the close of it. Twenty-one years, now, and it still seemed to be the biggest thing that had ever happened to the old farts who'd been caught up in it. Fellows who'd been firing away at each other at Cold Harbor, Second Manassas, the Wilderness, all those dinky places back East, they'd hunker down by the trail fire at night and go over old times—easier to talk to a former enemy than to the younger ones who didn't know and didn't give a damn, he guessed. But, Jesus, it was time to let it go by now. It was over, and it had never had much to do with the West, anyhow. He hoped Sieber wouldn't turn out to be one of the kind that was always dragging out old combat stories.

His new employer relieved his mind on that point, for the moment, by abandoning the War of the Rebellion and saying, "What I hear, you got a right to that name."

"Horn?" He shook his head slightly, feeling that something had got past him.

Sieber laughed and said, "Maybe. Your business anyhow, that is. I mean, what the Apache call you, the Talking Boy. You know their talk, Navaho language, some Spanish, huh?"

"Yah."

Sieber studied him. "You don't look like a student kind of fellow. How come you know these languages?"

"Oh . . ." He took another slug from the bottle and rested it again on the saddle in front of him. "You go in places where people are talking, makes sense to know what they're saying. Not that tough to puzzle out. People talk a lot, but, come down to it, they don't say very much, and it ain't hard, most times, to figure what they're trying to get across. I mean, a Mex points a gun at you and says something, you just give a good listen to what he says, and you got the Spanish for 'Hands up!'" He gestured with the bottle. "'S like that. Just listen."

Sieber regarded him thoughtfully. "And don't talk more than what you can help, huh?"

Horn said, "I see more fellows that made money or kept a whole skin by keeping a closed mouth than by tellin' all they knew." He gestured with the bottle. "Okay, a few drinks with a friend now and then, get a load off of . . . wherever you got a load, huh? Trade a few brags and such, why not? But promiscuous talkin', to hear yourself talk, why that don't strike me as any better idea 'n pissing into the wind."

"So." Sieber tilted his bottle. "You in the mood for

some unloadings, a brag or so? You know, Mr. Horn, I hear lots of things about you, I got to figure half of them probably true, so it's worth taking you on, but I don't know which half."

Horn shrugged. "Ain't much. Bummed my way west when I was fourteen, worked on the Santa Fe lines, stage driver and rider for the Overland Mail, herded oxen for some teamsters, horse herding for the Army, put in some time living with some of the tribes, ranch work here and there." He lifted the bottle and drank again.

"A lot of jobs," Sieber said. "How come? You find you ain't so good at one, you pull out and go on to another?"

Horn reined up his horse and glared at Sieber. "I'll tell you somethin', Mister Chief Scout Al Sieber. I ain't never done anything that I wasn't better at—not when I was fourteen, even—than any man around me. A while before I run off from home, my pa whipped the shit out of me, as was his right, being my pa, and he may be a better man than me if he's still alive, I won't say he is or isn't better, but if he is, he's the only damn one. What I done in my life so far maybe ain't any great shakes, but you're not gonna find anyone who's done it any better."

His momentary anger was spent now, and he shook his head ruefully. "But about that moving on, I dunno. Seems as if you get to do something real well, then there ain't any reason to go on doing it. I get to feeling, after I been in a job a while, that I'm not going to get any better at it, 'cause by then I'm doing it as well as it can be done, just get older. So . . ." He shrugged and took another drink from the bottle.

"Well," Sieber said, "the kind of job you got with me, you don't *get* to get older unless you keep getting better, so maybe you be hanging around a while." He raised his bottle in a here's-to-you gesture and drank.

CHAPTER 3

Horn was up first, out of his blankets and making the cook fire before the sun topped the flat horizon. He prided himself on what he thought of as a clock inside him; he could pick any time at all, even half-past two in the morning for a night trail watch, and be awake on the button. Nobody had ever had to grab him by the shoulder and shake him into consciousness, and a damn good thing, too, he thought—the man that did that stood a good chance of taking a slug from the gun Horn always kept within reach as he slept.

He looked around, taking in the white-hot rim of the sun just coming into view, the high, clear sky taking on the color of the day, the grove of trees near which they'd camped; he savored the chill of the morning air and the growing heat of the fire as he carefully built it up from a few glowing twigs. A *damn* fine morning to be on your way someplace. . . .

Sieber pawed his way out of his blankets and sat up, preserving a kind of rough dignity even in the gray suit of long underwear he'd slept in. He gritted his teeth as he jerked at his right leg with hands locked behind the knee, loosening it up for the day.

Horn, still crouching, tensed. "Al?" he said softly.

19

Sieber looked at him.

"Indians."

Sieber was suddenly very still. "Where?"

"Trees. Four of 'em."

Stretching, Sieber, with careful casualness, turned his head. The lower branches on the small stand of trees formed an intricate pattern, masking anything behind them; but Sieber had long since trained himself to disregard such camouflage. Squinting, he could make out the motionless forms of four men hidden among the trees. He let his glance range farther, then gave an elaborate yawn and said quietly, "Five."

Horn looked at him questioningly. "Behind the far bush," Sieber murmured.

Horn moved around the fire until he was facing the bush, and took a quick glance at it. Right . . . another one. He remembered ruefully his boast of the day before to Sieber. Being able to do anything he did better than anyone around him was mostly true, but at this moment he didn't have one idea about what was going on or what to do about it. This stuff was Sieber's trade, and it was time he came up with some clever notions. Right now, the legendary scout was pulling his pants on, which was sensible enough, Horn considered, but not much contribution to solving the problem. Sieber had better think of something good. . . .

"Sing 'Life's Railway to Heaven,' " Sieber said.

"*What*?" If hymn singing was in order, Horn thought, "Nearer, My God, to Thee" would have fit the circumstances better. But what the *hell* . . . ?

"I sing *horrible*," Sieber muttered furiously. "Everything must look *natural*—goddammit, *sing*!"

Horn grimaced, but cut some bacon from the slab he had set out into a frying pan and set it on the fire while he tried to recall how the song began.

" 'Life is like a mountain railroad,' " he sang mournfully.

" 'With an engineer that's brave. We must make the run successful'—They hostiles or friendly?"

"I don't think either—keep singing."

" '—from the cradle to the grave.' "

"If they was friendly, they'd probably be closer; if they was hostiles, we'd probably be dead."

" 'Put your trust alone in Jesus,' " Horn sang as bacon snapped and twisted in the pan and he nudged a battered coffeepot in to rest on the fire's coals. " 'Never falter, never fail.' What's going *on*, Al?"

Sieber gritted his teeth and jerked harder at his stiff leg. "Don't call me Al, keep singing."

" 'Keep your hand upon the throttle
" 'And your eye upon the rail.' "

Contrary to the hymn's injunction, Horn had his eye upon the bush that concealed the last Indian and, as he concluded the verse, saw a powerful, bronzed figure in buckskin leggings and vest step from behind it. The warrior called out to him in Apache.

Sieber said, "You're the Talking Boy, go on, go on, what'd he say?"

Horn gave the rumpled figure of Sieber, pants still unbuttoned and upper torso swathed in dingy gray homespun, a sardonic glance. "His chief has sent him to speak to the mighty man of iron."

"I'm here," Sieber said. "Tell him to get on with it."

Horn pulled the frying pan from the fire and set it to one side. He stood up, raised his right hand, palm outward, and, trying for his deepest chest tones, asked what the warror and his four evidently modest companions wanted with the iron man. He listened to the burst of Apache that followed, then turned to Sieber. "His chief says the final war is soon to start."

Sieber nodded.

Horn went on, "His chief warns not to join the chase against him. If you join the chase against him, his chief will have to kill you, which would make him very sad."

Sieber hit his leg with the edge of his palm and gave a grunt of mingled pain and satisfaction, then muttered, "It would not fill me with much joy either." He squinted across to where the Indian stood. "Tell his chief I have to track him. I may not always like it, but it's my job."

Horn called the message across. The warrior received it with neither comment nor any movement; the four other Indians also remained immobile.

Horn mulled over the messages he had been receiving and transmitting and realized that there were elements in them that made him uneasy. That business about "the final war" sounded as if it would be mighty . . . *final* for a lot of the fellows involved in it, and Sieber seemed to be a prime target for whatever old buck he was trailing—which meant that Sieber's assistant was standing right in the bull's-eye, too. "Who's his chief?" he asked after a moment, still keeping an eye on the motionless Indians.

Sieber's bad leg was stretched out, and he looked

up at Horn as he massaged the kneecap. "Geronimo, Mr. Horn; the one and only."

Horn pushed the pan of partly cooked bacon back onto the fire. *Geronimo.* A man gets tired of making cows go from one place to another and takes a job that might have a bit more interest to it . . . and next thing you know, he gets word he's in a tangle with Geronimo. Like some Ohio boy who was made colonel of his volunteer regiment because his pa had the money to buy uniforms for the outfit being told he's to try conclusions with Robert E. Lee, come morning. They didn't come any shrewder than Geronimo, nor any crueler. Talk about an interesting job, this *had* to be it. Horn flicked a glance at Sieber, who was now shrugging into a worn wool shirt, and told himself, Okay, so it's Geronimo. Comes to being mean and smart, I guess I can match him.

He checked the bacon in the pan and withdrew it from the fire just at the point at which it had turned brown and chewy—well off the raw but not burned, bacon the way it should be. At the same time, as he had planned it, the coffeepot came to a boil and was set aside to bubble and cool. Not so much to cooking, if you paid any mind to what you were doing, never mind what the trail cooks said about it, but it was plain dumb, if you were doing it at all, not to do it just right.

"They're gone, Mr. Horn," Sieber said. "They gave me their message—the four who said nothing as much as the one who spoke—and they went away. Our hair's still on, for a while. Breakfast ready?"

"Accourse it is," Horn said, and began shoveling bacon onto two tin plates.

CHAPTER 4

The sky stretched overhead like a huge blue bowl. To Horn, riding beside but just a little behind Sieber, it seemed perfect and changeless. Sieber, though, appeared to find something of special interest in it, low down and off to his left. Horn followed the direction of his gaze and saw a faint smudge of pale gray above the trees on a low hill just ahead. Trail dust, that would be, and from a fair number of horses.

Sieber changed course and headed for the dust smudge, urging his horse to greater speed. Horn followed. They rode through the stand of trees and paused at the rim of the hill. A little more than half a mile off, Horn could see a file of men dressed in dusty blue heading southwest.

"Patrol," Sieber said. "Second Cavalry, out of Bowie." He squinted. "The officer, there; see him?" Horn picked out a glint of silver flashing from the shoulder of a man slightly bigger than the others, and nodded. "By his size, that'd be Lawton. Good in the saddle, because that's where his brains is. We better go see what he's up to."

The patrol was not making much speed, and Horn and Sieber caught up with it in ten minutes. Lieutenant Lawton—handsome as well as big, Horn noticed, looking as though he'd been raised on some government stud farm for thoroughbred officers—greeted them warmly.

"I'm glad to see you, Sieber," he said. "We need all the guns we can get." He nudged his horse closer to Sieber's and dropped his voice. "Two of Geronimo's best men have broken with him," he said impressively. He pointed to the head of the short column, where two Indians in Apache dress rode in company with three scouts in civilian clothes. "They're taking us to where he's camped. By George, we'll have the old fox before he knows it!"

Sieber's eyes narrowed as he looked at Lawton's two informants. "Lieutenant Lawton, that's Dandy Jim and Deadshot—two of his closest friends."

Lawton nodded happily. "I told you they were his best men. Where were you headed, to Bowie?"

"We were."

"Well, you stay with me now." He gave them a wave and rode ahead.

"There is three kinds of peoples in this world," Sieber said dreamily, watching the tall figure on the high-stepping horse. "There is colored peoples, and there is white peoples, and there is assholes." He pointed a stubby finger at Lawton. "All soldiers is assholes."

Horn said nothing. Sieber seemed to have summed it up well enough.

The scout glanced at him. "Now, Talking Boy, I think maybe it's time you get to work. But better you be *listening* boy than talking boy just now, you understand?" He nodded toward the head of the column.

25

"Right," Horn said. He rode past the plodding cavalrymen, noticing that Lawton was occupied in seeing that the spacing between the riders was kept uniform, and came up to the two Apaches, now a little ahead of the other riders.

"How," he said with a broad smile, raising his right hand. It occurred to him that he had never heard any Indian of any tribe say "How" under any circumstances, except a Chiricahua once, who had wanted to know the principle of the telegraph. Maybe the ones the half-dime novel writers knew were a different crowd.

The two Apaches looked at him without interest.

Horn pointed at Deadshot's moccasins. "Wantum sellum?"

The Indians' lack of interest seemed to deepen. Horn pulled some coins from his pocket and displayed them; with his other hand he pointed to his boots. "My . . . boots," he said, mouthing the words with exaggerated distinctness, "too *heavy*." He grimaced and hunched in the saddle, trying to *look* heavy. "So *me*"—he pointed at his chest—"me wantum buyum *your*"—he pointed at Deadshot—"your mocca-sins." He favored them with a broad, foolish smile. "Yes?"

Dandy Jim and Deadshot had said nothing throughout Horn's attempt at commerce, but now, still ignoring him, talked quickly between themselves in their own language. Their faces were not expressive, but they appeared to find something amusing in what they were saying.

Horn, still smiling widely, continued to hold his money out, and continued to be ignored. After a few moments, he said, "No? Me sorry. We talkum other time, maybe you sellum then. So longum."

He waved at the Apaches and dropped back until he was riding beside Sieber once again.

"What'd they say?" the scout asked. "It is an ambush?"

"Could be."

"They say where?"

"Cibucu Canyon. Anyhow, they were saying that the weak-footed one wouldn't need boots *or* moccasins to get out of Cibucu, the vultures'd be taking him out, bite by bite, along with the horse soldiers. They seemed to think it was a pretty good joke."

"It ain't everybody can appreciate the Apache sense of humor," Sieber said, and spurred his horse ahead until he caught up with Lawton. The lieutenant was not impressed with Sieber's news.

"I don't propose to cancel a military operation because you tell me somebody I never laid eyes on until an hour ago overheard a couple of Apaches joking between themselves, Sieber. Of course an ambush is a possibility, it's always a possibility, but what if you're wrong and it isn't? I cannot pass up a chance like this."

"Well, at *least* take some precautions," Sieber said, controlling his exasperation with difficulty.

"Fine," Lawton said. "I'll send six men out on the flanks, if that makes you feel any better."

Sieber looked at him disgustedly. Lawton had just come up with a perfectly sensible cavalry-manual solution to the problem, well suited to maneuvers and battles on the broad plains of Europe; it was a damn shame that he just happened to be leading a cavalry patrol in the canyon country of Arizona against an enemy who wasn't working from the same manual. "It doesn't," he said. "*None* of this does."

"That's because you're a civilian and not a soldier," Lawton said loftily. "Sieber, personally I don't have much against you, but . . . you know the truth and so do I." His tone was confidential now.

Sieber closed his eyes briefly. Lawton the textbook soldier was hard enough to take; Lawton being man-to-man was worse.

"Once Geronimo's captured," the lieutenant went on smugly, "*our* work is done, and we get shipped some place better. But all you *civilian* employees, once he's captured . . . hell, *you're* broke and out of a job." An officer's dignity does not allow him to wink, but Lawton's glance at Sieber had a knowing quality that came close to winking, letting the scout know that a holder of the President's commission could understand that civilians, being without honor, were prone to moneygrubbing, but that he didn't propose to condone it.

Sieber scowled, whirled his horse around, and rode back toward Horn.

Dandy Jim and Deadshot had observed but not overheard the exchange between the officer and the scout, and stiffened slightly in their saddles at Lawton's barked orders that sent flankers out. But when they saw that the column's direction remained unchanged, they relaxed once more.

In the later afternoon, the character of the country changed, becoming rockier and broken; the sparse grass gave way to stony expanses and barren, wind-eroded hills.

Sieber squinted ahead and saw Lawton, riding at the head of the column behind the two Apaches, reach down and touch the rifle scabbarded at his side. "Nearer we get, the surer he ain't that it's not an ambush," Sieber muttered to Horn. "But he's not going to stop and think it over, maybe look into why he might of been wrong in the first place. Wouldn't be *soldierly*."

Horn said nothing.

Reaching a ledge that overhung a dry river bed, Deadshot and Dandy Jim halted and beckoned for Lawton. When he reached them, they pointed at the rim of the ledge, then rode along it to where a fall of weathered rock made a slope down to the river bed. Lawton paused a moment, reassured himself once again of his rifle's presence, then sent his horse after them, followed by the cavalry column.

"Where Cibucu begins," Sieber said. He looked around at the lengthening shadows; the westering sun painted the rock a bright red. He looked closely at Horn. "Ever been in an Indian battle?"

Horn shook his head.

"Ever kill anyone?"

Horn's negative gesture was quick and abrupt.

"Then you got to do what I tell you." He turned and gestured toward the soldiers riding ahead of them. A short figure in disgracefully sloppy civilian clothes dropped out of the column and waited for them. Horn studied him and wondered what Sieber had in mind. Swarthy, with a face like a comic-paper Irishman, bright red hair, one piercing blue eye matched by a seamed socket, and perhaps, when afoot, five foot tall, the man looked outlandish but unimpressive.

"Micky Free," Sieber muttered. "Irish papa, Apache mother, best damn scout ever."

"How'd he come to lose that eye, then?" Horn asked.

"Deer hooked it out when he was twelve. He sees better with that one eye than you 'n me do with two."

They were now up to where Free sat his horse, smiling broadly. "Mr. Horn, Mr. Free," Sieber said.

Horn nodded. "Afternoon."

Micky Free's smile widened, but he did not return the greeting.

"Mr. Free isn't much on talking," Sieber said. He looked intently at Horn. "You *stay* with Mr. Free."

Free nodded cheerfully.

"You stay *right* with him. Whatever he does, you do. Wherever he goes, you stay right alongside."

Horn studied the diminutive scout. He did not look like any great shakes as a combat companion. "Why?"

Sieber lowered his voice portentously. "*He can't get killed.*" He raised one hand to forestall Horn's incredulous response. "I *know* it's crazy, but I been through too much with him. Everybody for twenty feet around him down and dead in a fight, full of arrows as a pincushion, and him just grinning and shooting away, not even grazed. He can't get killed . . . and he knows it."

Sieber rode toward the head of the column as it wound down into the canyon, leaving Horn alone with Free. Horn moved his horse closer to the grinning, silent half-breed's mount. From what Dandy Jim and Deadshot had been saying, it looked as though being next to someone unkillable could be a good idea pretty damned soon.

CHAPTER 5

Horn edged his horse close to Micky Free's as they entered the canyon. He didn't know anything about military tactics, but it struck him that the Cibucu looked like a better place to be out of than in if you were expecting trouble. The sloping, rocky walls formed a shallow vee, with the advancing cavalry nicely positioned in the bottom point. The three flankers on either side, now lost to sight as they moved through the sparse growth at the top, might smoke out any lurking hostiles; then again, they might not. Horn did not feel very confident that they would.

The crumbling rock of the dry river bed sent up clouds of dust as the horses' hoofs disturbed it; Horn, at the rear of the column, got the full, choking benefit of the dust, and thought longingly of the two bottles of Old Brigham remaining in his saddlebags. But it wouldn't do, he supposed, to take a snort just now; it would be best to be a little on edge until they were through the canyon.

Horn squinted ahead and saw Lawton, leading the column, reach down again and stroke his rifle. In the middle of the cavalry, Sieber unsheathed his own rifle and held it loosely, looking from one side of the canyon to the other in a constant sweep.

The canyon was still, except for the somehow muted noises of a troop of cavalry moving at a walk— not even a bird call or the scuttling sound of a startled lizard. The sun still lit the canyon top, but the riders were moving in deepening shadow, into an area of brush and dwarfed trees.

Horn glanced at Micky Free. The scout's grin was even wider, and his eye seemed to blaze. Whatever was going to happen, Horn thought, Free was ready for it. And so was he, he realized with mild surprise. But it would be nice to know just what the hell he was ready *for*. . . .

His eyes snapped to the front of the column as the rhythm of hoofbeats suddenly changed. The two Apaches were spurring their horses and racing ahead of the soldiers.

He had just time to register the picture clearly before the storm of gunfire swept the cavalry, from the rim of the canyon on their right and the brush and trees ahead. He caught a brief glimpse of one of the flankers against the skyline, slumping in his saddle.

In front of him, horses reared and men fell. Some had their weapons out and were returning fire into the shadows; he saw Sieber taking aim and firing, though there seemed to be no target in sight.

Beside him, Micky Free gave a long, gobbling yell that made the hair on the back of Horn's neck prickle, threw Horn a wide smile, and dug his spurs into his horse's flanks, sending the animal straight at the point where the firing was heaviest.

Horn said, "Shit!" and followed. Sieber had said to

stay with Micky Free, and Horn had nothing better to do right now, but it seemed to him that the little scout was putting a considerable strain on the legend about his not being capable of being killed.

Riding furiously after Micky Free, Horn saw a gut-shot horse directly in front of him stand almost straight up on its rear legs, screaming as it dumped its rider, then crashing down on him, squeezing a brief echoing scream from the man. Another cavalryman clapped both hands to a face that was suddenly a mask of red, and toppled from his mount.

It seemed to Horn weird that he was seeing these events unmoved, as though they were magic-lantern pictures projected on a wall. He had expected to be scared shitless, but the whole business was somehow impersonal—he, along with everybody else, was doing something that had to be worked out in a certain way, and what happened was what happened. Right now, he was supposed to be keeping up with Micky Free. The fellow under the horse and the one with no face were out of the game now, that was all that amounted to. He was aware that bullets were going past Tom Horn, and that any one of them might go into or through him, but he was not quite sure who Tom Horn was. He was in charge of Horn, though, and had to see that he did whatever he was doing in the best way.

It was oddly easy to send his horse dodging around the welter of rearing, whirling horses and men and keep close to Free; it was as though he could with no effort see ahead to where a falling horse or a running man would be by the time he got there.

He was now almost up to Sieber and saw with approval that he was pushing the cavalrymen from their horses, urging them to get on foot where they would make less of a target. Blood blossomed on Sieber's shoulder, and he reeled in his saddle. Horn felt a flood of irritation, which subsided as Sieber pulled himself upright and continued his task; it wouldn't be *right* for Sieber to drop out of the fight now, while he still had work to do.

The dust was blinding, choking, and Horn's irritation returned. Nobody ever said anything about dust in battles—it was shooting and such that it was all supposed to be about. Dust was a needless complication.

He was interested to see, emerging from the dust cloud, a huge Indian on a horse, holding a giant war club already in a downswing nicely calculated to dash Horn's brains out. The fast sideward slide that took him half out of the saddle and the jab of spurs into his horse's side that sent the animal leaping ahead were easy to figure out and execute; the blow swung past him, and he was into the dust cloud again.

Micky Free was only a little in front of him; but now he saw Deadshot and Dandy Jim riding up the left-hand slope of the canyon wall, getting clear of the dust and the fighting. It surprised him that they had not got much farther away; the fight seemed to have been going on for a long time. Once the two renegades were at the canyon rim, they would be in a commanding position to set up a crossfire down into the disordered cavalry, with the sun at their backs making counterfire almost impossible; it seemed to Horn more important to do something about that than to stay with Micky Free.

Horn cut through the melee, spurring his horse to a speed he would normally have avoided on this treacherous ground, guiding it with preternatural sureness around obstacles that might have made it stumble; Dandy Jim and Deadshot, picking their way more slowly up the slope, grew larger in his sight.

Then he was off the comparatively level ground of the canyon bottom and beginning to climb; the horse's pace slowed. Impatiently, he grabbed his rifle, pistol, and ammunition and vaulted from the saddle to the ground, propelling himself ahead with the horse's forward momentum even as the animal hit a loose rock and went down on its knees.

Horn was elated at the power that seemed to be running through him, clarifying his vision and his mind. Hand- and footholds sprang into his sight as he needed them, then took his weight and propelled him upward, as if he himself had little or nothing to do with the process. Reach—grab—push off . . . he seemed to be flung up the slope like a missile fired from a weapon, not climbing it with laboring breath, with bleeding palms and in a sweaty stench of anger and panic.

Jagged rocks cut the Indians off from his view as he climbed; then suddenly Dandy Jim was alone in front of him—Deadshot had angled off, then, probably to the left, *okay*, time enough for him after . . .

Horn seemed to be looking down on the scene from a height, seeing everything with an uncanny clarity. The running man bounded after the mounted one, flipping his rifle end over end, fitting both hands to the barrel, raising the stock in a lazy sweep—given extra impetus by his forward leap—that crunched into the base of the Apache's skull. Dandy Jim toppled from his horse with a single choked scream, hit the shaley slope, and rolled down toward the canyon bottom, arms and legs flopping loosely like a flung rag doll's.

Horn angled left around his victim's confused horse and ran along a narrow rock outcropping. As he had figured, there ahead of him was Deadshot, spurring and beating his mount to scramble up the last few feet to the canyon rim, then turning to see the vengeful pursuing figure. Horn seemed not so much to jump as to flow to the back of the horse, settling onto it and crooking an arm in a stranglehold around the Apache's neck. Then the sky and ground tilted, and the linked men slid from the back of the rearing, panicked horse, to smash onto the ground.

Horn felt a tightness in his head and a stinging smell of dust in his nostrils; then a moccasined foot slammed into his face as Deadshot, wrenching free, got in the first blow. He was aware that he was stunned, but that seemed to make no difference to his automatic response, bringing the rifle up like a baseball bat and around in a satisfying swing that felt *just* right, hitting the skull with a solid cracking sound, feeling it go just that little bit past the point of contact that meant that Deadshot was off the board permanently, and, sure enough, there the damn fool went, skidding down the slope, open eyes already filming with dust. . . .

Horn rolled to his feet, sprang the last few steps to the rim, slid onto his belly, and sent a volley from his revolver into the densest patch of scrub on the opposite wall of the canyon—that was where the heaviest fire had been coming from. He alternated between the revolver and the rifle, shooting and reloading, until he was aware that there was no more fire coming from across the canyon.

Out of the shadows, he saw Sieber leading some of the surviving cavalrymen up the lower reaches of the slope he had climbed. They were not far away, but they seemed distant, still viewed with that same detached clarity that had been with him throughout the fight. He could see the glance of contempt that Sieber flung at the unhorsed and tattered Lieutenant Lawton, and the dimming of Micky Free's smile as the half-breed scout realized that the afternoon's fun was over.

Now Sieber was close to him, dismounting, approaching the rim. Horn leaned over, grasped his hand, and gave him a tug to help him up to the top.

Sieber said nothing for a moment, just looked at him intently. Horn felt as if his whole body and mind were like a leg that had gone to sleep and was now fizzing and tingling as circulation returned. He was aware of where he was, but just now was not sure how he had got there and what he had been doing; he could remember individual actions, but had no sense of how or why he had performed them.

"You took position," Sieber said slowly.

"Hmm?" Horn said.

"Just now."

Horn shrugged. "I just beat 'em up the hill, is all." That was the closest he could come to it; the Indians had been going up the hill, and it had been somehow up to him to beat them. The dreamlike clearness of vision and certainty of decision were fading now.

"True," Sieber said. "But nobody else beat 'em up the hill. I said stay with Mr. Free, but instead you overtook two of Geronimo's best men and . . ." He looked downslope to where Deadshot and Dandy Jim lay sprawled at the end of separate paths of scattered stones. ". . . kind of helped end things."

Horn looked at him with vague interest, then turned and began to walk away.

"Dammit, I'm not done with you!" Sieber called, his tone sharpened by a twinge from his shoulder wound. Horn stopped and Sieber limped toward him. "I asked about you before hiring. 'Horn?' they said. 'The White Indian?' they said. 'Be careful, you never know with him.' No close friends, lots of enemies. That true?"

Horn considered this dispassionately. "I guess."

Sieber's face was lit by the sun, now almost below the horizon, as he leaned toward Horn and asked, "*Why* don't people like you?"

Horn reached for an answer, while his gaze idly swept the canyon below, taking in the still figures of the dead and the moving or resting cavalrymen and horses, recalling the exciting strangeness of the fight, and how little of what happened to any of them, even to Tom Horn, had seemed to matter at the time. . . .

"I don't know," he said at last. "They never have."

CHAPTER 6

Horn was firmly of the opinion that he did not like hospital visits. Maybe a real hospital would be different from an Army one set up in a tent at Fort Bowie, but probably not much. It wasn't likely that the smells of carbolic acid and sickly sweet medicines, of bedridden men the orderlies hadn't got to in time, of festering wounds, would be any different, or that there would be any fewer whimpers and moans, or, worst of all, that thin thread of chuckling that drifted to him from some corner of the tent he couldn't see and didn't want to. The only difference between this and a civilian hospital was that everyone being treated in Fort Bowie's medical haven this day was there as a direct result of Lieutenant Henry Lawton being an asshole, and Horn couldn't see that that made the atmosphere any better or worse. The plain fact was that he didn't like to be around people who were hurting and letting it be known that they hurt.

Sieber, at least, wasn't hurting badly, or anyhow not showing it, which came to the same thing. Sitting on a cot, he clenched his teeth as the young medical orderly, a private—a gentle-looking kid, but with something awfully old around the eyes—cleaned out his wound, but didn't groan or yell. Horn tried to work out whether it took more guts to have your torn flesh and muscle swabbed at, or to do the swabbing, and decided he would be best off not having to make the choice.

"We never got to use up the Old Brigham on the way back here," he said to Sieber. "You get done with this, we can set ourselves up for some relaxing. Two bottles each, we got still."

Sweat stood out on Sieber's face as he replied. "Yah. Lucky we got them, else I think I ask you to get a twelve-pound sledge from the farrier and give me a nice tap alongside the head, so I wake up maybe Thursday and all this pig-dog pain's got a chance to die down, Jesu Mareeeeyahl"

"Thass got it," the private said, pulling taut and knotting the thread he had been using to stitch Sieber's wound, an operation which had elicited the scout's yelped appeal to divinity. "You'll be right as rain pret' soon, no proud flesh into that atall, an' I scraped away all the dirt an' crap."

"I remember you did that," Sieber said heavily.

Someone at the far end of the tent was loudly anxious for his mother to be there; Horn wondered what benefit the woman would derive from seeing her son at the point of an extremely painful death. During the fight, there hadn't been any stuff like this; it had been just Go *here*, Do *this*, Stay away from *that* . . . this leftover stuff, with the blood and pus and hurting and fear and reaching for comfort, that was all pretty messy and made him uneasy. Horn wondered who, if he'd been shot through the body and known he wasn't going to make it, he'd have called for. Pa, Ma, anybody? Nobody, come down to it. Maybe old Shed, tail threshing back and forth and whuffling like a steam engine . . . Shed would come up and lick his face if Horn was dying, as if he was hoping he could make everything all right. But Shed was a tangle of bare bones back in Missouri, killed for no reason a dozen years back by some shithead emigrant passing through. Likely he'd have been dead by now, anyhow; dogs didn't last all that long.

A flash of light from the front of the tent told him that the entry flap had been opened and shut; he looked toward it and saw a bizarre figure wandering in. It was that of a man well into middle age, clad in a rumpled canvas suit, his seamed face bounded by a beard and mustache below and a wide-brimmed hat of floppily oriental construction above. Horn wondered what business this weird character might have in the hospital; God help all there if he was one of the doctors. Disquietingly, the apparition looked toward them and called out, "Al?"

Horn gave an involuntary start as Sieber said, "Yes, General?"

"That's a *general*?" he whispered, watching the untidy—hell, he thought, speak the truth and shame the devil, the bugger is downright sloppy—figure approached them.

"General Crook," Sieber muttered. "The best."

Horn, if he had been given to that sort of gesture, would have pursed his lips in a silent whistle. Major General George A. Crook did indeed have the name of being the best of the men Washington had sent out to pacify the Indians, one of the few who took the trouble to find out something about them other than how they were at fighting. He was not Horn's idea of what an officer looked like, but, considering how the spit-and-polish Lawton had turned out, that might be all to the good.

Crook came up to the cot where Sieber sat and spoke to him gruffly. "Don't you know any better than to get ambushed?"

"Getting old, General," Sieber said. "I look like a kid, but I'm not anymore."

Crook jerked a thumb toward Horn. "This the one got position?" Sieber nodded. "That was good. Taking the hill."

"I was mainly interested in saving my ass," Horn said. He had not told Sieber about the curious dream-like state in which he had gone through the battle, and didn't propose to mention it to the general.

"Always a laudable occupation," Crook said. "Basic element of the military art."

The young private finished dressing Sieber's wound and moved on to the patient on the next cot. Sieber began pulling his shirt on, wincing but managing it well enough.

Crook was dead serious as he spoke again. "You got to promise me to bring in Geronimo."

"He surrenders when he wants to," Sieber said. "We both know that. I can punish him some, keep pressuring, make it hard for him, but that's about all."

The general looked at him intently. "I'll promise you any supplies you need, you promise me you'll capture him."

"No." It was flat and final.

Crook gave him a bitter look. "Everybody says, 'The great Al Sieber.' I say, what's so damn great about him?" Sieber said nothing, and the general's shoulders slumped. "They're eating me alive in Washington, Al."

Sieber finished buttoning his shirt. "Figured."

"Grover Cleveland wants Geronimo, that's what it all comes down to." Crook shook his head. "The first Democratic President elected in twenty-five years and he wants re-election and Geronimo's the last of the hostiles. He gets captured, that makes the West look safe. The West looks safe, that makes Cleveland look good."

Crook grimaced in disgust and started to move to the next cot, whose occupant had now been dealt with by the medical orderly. He stopped and addressed Sieber again. "Geronimo's headed into Mexico and if I can't bring him out and make him surrender, the word is out. Washington's going to send down General Miles to do the job." He gave Sieber a long look, then turned to the wounded soldier.

Horn saw that Sieber's face was distorted in a scowl. "How bad is Miles?" he asked.

Sieber looked up at him. "There is four kinds of people in this world. Colored peoples, white peoples, assholes, and General Miles."

Horn had expected, not giving it much thought, that he and Sieber would be quartered in barracks; but the civilian scouts were allotted tents in an area of the fort well away from the regular troops. "They need us," Sieber said, "but they don't understand us or like us. We are civilians, which is bad enough, but my scouts is Indians, which is worse. All most soldiers want to know about Indians is how to shoot them, which is what my scouts is supposed to help them to do, but that don't seem to make no difference."

Horn was just as glad for the isolation from the troops. He suspected that military discipline would frown on the way he, Sieber, and Micky Free were spending the evening. Free was already dead drunk, lying happily by the small fire outside their tent; Horn was unhurriedly working on achieving the same state, and contentedly braiding lengths of fine cord to form a long rope. His old lariat was good enough, but he had worked out a way to form an even more supple rope, and was interested in trying it out. A man gets satisfied with "good enough," he thought vaguely, taking another pull at the bottle, and pretty soon he isn't good for much. Once you see how a thing could be better, only makes sense to do it that way.

Sieber came into the circle of firelight, holding his own bottle of Old Brigham, and sat next to Horn. He looked pleased, Horn observed—first time this day since his talk with General Crook.

"Got some word from the adjutant," he said. "Emmet Crawford's going to lead us into Mexico. Should be here day after tomorrow."

"That good?" Horn said, his fingers still moving deftly, almost automatically.

"He's a great fighting man," Sieber said. He tipped the bottle up and gulped, then exhaled gustily. "Must be a colonel by now. Big. A bull. Once, when we was chasing Loco, the Apaches caught us in a rock slide . . ." He looked sharply at Horn, who was now again intent on his rope braiding. "Interested?"

"I got nothing else to do till I get drunk," Horn said.

Sieber's eyes narrowed a little, but he continued. "Anyway, after the slide, Crawford said, 'I'm okay, are you?' And I said, 'Well, my bad leg is now my good leg,' and Crawford had to carry me five miles, maybe more." He hefted the bottle, decided there was enough left so that he did not have to ration the whiskey, and drank again. "I did Emmet some good turns, too, but I still owe him one. After what he done for me that day, I'll always owe him one. . . ."

He lifted his bottle once more; so did Horn. Sieber stared into the fire; Horn went back to braiding. His and Sieber's second bottles of whiskey would do to finish out the night, he calculated; that left one each to see them through until they went out with this Crawford. Good enough.

Horn, riding with Micky Free, pondered over the good things and the bad things about the mission. On the good side was the fact that it was not a standard cavalry operation; instead of soldiers, it was made up of thirty-some Indian scouts. Horn felt a lot more comfortable with men who knew what they were up to in this country. On the bad side, Lieutenant Lawton was the second-in-command. Evidently getting his men shot up because of his own stupidity didn't count against him enough to matter, to the Army way of thinking.

And Crawford . . . he shook his head. Hard to figure whether he was a plus or a minus. Sieber's dismay when he first saw his old comrade-in-arms had been evident. First off, the big officer's shoulders had sported only the twin bars of a captain, no oak leaves or eagles, as the scout had predicted.

And beyond that—no, not beyond, it had to be tied in with it—there was that burned-out look he had. Big, well-set-up, pleasant-looking . . . but hollow inside. He knew his stuff, that was easy to see, but what he'd do in a pinch, that wasn't easy to guess. . . .

Horn let the thoughts drift away from him. No use to speculate, anyhow. He'd find out when the time came.

Ahead of the motley crew of Indian scouts Lawton rode alone. Ahead of him rode Sieber and Crawford. They were silent, and Sieber found himself glancing more and more often at his friend, waiting for the moment when it would be all right to say something, but not finding it.

He shrugged, turned in his saddle, and bawled back toward the rear of the untidy column, "Mr. Horn!"

To Horn, riding up a moment later, Sieber seemed ill at ease, falsely jovial as he spoke to Crawford. "We're soon entering Mexico and Mr. Horn is new at this, so naturally he should be worried and I thought this would relax him some." He turned to Horn. "See, there's never been a team like me and Crawford." His head swiveled toward the officer. "Who didn't we catch?" he said heartily. "Chato, we missed him, now who else?"

Crawford, staring straight ahead, did not seem to be aware that Sieber was talking, or even that he was there.

"Cochise we never even got close to," Sieber said with a forced chuckle. "Who else?" Horn could see a kind of desperation beginning to grow in him. "*Nana*," Sieber said hurriedly. "We didn't get him, too, and he was over eighty! Who else?" Crawford remained silent.

Sieber turned to Horn. "It's not important, just remember, you shouldn't worry, look who's on your side. The world's oldest Indian scout . . . and the Army's most experienced captain!"

Sieber's joke finally got a response from the officer—a quick turn of the head, a long stare, and a sudden pressure of knees and spurs that sent his horse pounding ahead.

Alone with Horn, Sieber pulled a bandana from his pocket and mopped his face, continuing long after the sweat should have been absorbed. Horn said nothing but found himself throwing a sideward glance at the scout, looking ahead to the trail, and back to Sieber again—much, though he did not know it, as Sieber himself had been looking at Crawford. It made Horn uneasy to see Sieber so much at a loss . . . some rust patches on the Man of Iron. . . .

The column plodded through the heat until, with the sun enough past the zenith to cast shadows a little off the vertical, they came to an area of tumbled boulders where, with some effort and ingenuity, shade could be found, and Crawford called a rest halt.

Horn and Sieber sought the shelter of a medium-sized boulder and crouched to get the benefit of its shadow. The edge of the shadow suddenly changed shape and enlarged; Horn looked up and saw Crawford leaning on the boulder and looking down at them—looking, but, it seemed to him, not really seeing them.

As if continuing a conversation that had been started some time ago, Crawford said, "I had the au-

47

dacity to . . . to dispute a general over . . ." His face tightened, and his mouth twisted as he spoke the next word. ". . . *tac*tics. But that wasn't my mistake, you see, and it also wasn't that the dispute happened in front of a group of my fellow officers. No, my error was simply this—I turned out to be right."

He stepped from behind the rock, reached into the side pocket of his uniform jacket, and drew out a hammer-finished silver flask. Not taking his eyes from Horn and Sieber, and still seeming not to see them, he unscrewed the cap and drank from the flask. Horn thought that he might have offered to pass it around, but decided that Crawford's need was greater than his.

"So I did *not* become a major and the first time, I considered it an oversight, but the next time I was passed over I knew I would never become one. And now there are colonels I consider children."

Horn carefully studied the ground in front of him. Lots of pebbles there, mostly on the reddish side. Pebbles weren't much to be interested in, but looking at them was better than looking at Crawford's face, right now.

Sieber craned his head to stare at his friend. "Why didn't you resign, Emmet?"

Crawford glared at him. "And do what, Al? *And do what?*" The flask sent spears of sunlight stabbing down into the boulder's shadow as the captain tilted it high and held it to his mouth for a long moment.

CHAPTER 7

The border between Arizona Territory and the Republic of Mexico was not marked in any way, and Horn was not sure just when the column crossed it. Mexico or America, it was rocky going, and promising to get rockier as the Sierra Madres loomed to the south.

The third day into Mexico, Sieber put into operation the plan he had worked out with Crawford. "We'll cut in ahead," he said to Crawford. "Emmet, you head due south ten, make it fifteen, days. Wait a week. You should pick up some old men, maybe some squaws with children."

"You'll be able to link up with us by then?" the captain asked.

Sieber gave a slight nod. "I hope." He gave Crawford and the Indian scouts a sketchy wave of his right hand—Lawton, sitting his horse self-importantly to one side, could consider himself included in the gesture or not, it didn't matter a rat's ass to Sieber—and rode toward the mountains. Horn and Micky Free followed him. They were not a dignified procession, being mounted now on mules, with Micky Free leading an extra mule loaded with supplies, but Horn was

49

glad of the change. For mountain work, you wanted mules; they were too dumb to know when to be scared, or maybe too smart; anyhow, they kept whatever minds they had on putting their feet right and not falling off some ledge, while a horse was likely to get notional and panicky in that kind of situation, and wind up by plunging down a mountainside along with anybody luckless enough to be on his back at the time.

They headed for the higher ground as Crawford led his party south on a route that skirted the mountains. The going became tough almost immediately, and, intent on it, they did not look back to see Crawford's distant farewell wave.

All the way from Bowie it had been killingly hot, but by the time they made camp that first night they were high enough in the mountains for the chill to make their sleep fitful.

The second night was worse, and they slept huddled together for warmth. They awoke to find themselves and their belongings lightly dusted with snow.

"Early for snow," Horn observed.

"In these mountains, you get it early," Sieber said.

More often than not, now, they had to dismount and lead the mules up or down rocky, twisting paths. They were deep in the mountains, and it seemed to Horn that they might well be in another world. On every side they were hemmed in by cliffs and crags; when they emerged into the open it was only to see snowy peaks stretching away forever. Climbing and driving the mules up a treacherous slope was a back-breaking nightmare; going down, with their own weight threatening to overbalance them, was worse.

Horn wondered whether anything could be so important as to make all this necessary, but said nothing. Sieber wasn't complaining in spite of what the journey must be doing to his bad leg; and Micky Free was his usual silently cheerful self.

On the fifth day, Sieber studied an upward-winding path that lay ahead of them. "From here on," he said, "the going ain't as easy as it has been."

"I knew it was too good to last," Horn said.

"Hardly any place ahead you can ride more than five minutes at a time. The mules is no good to us after this except the pack one. We leave them here, get them later on, they got grazing and water in this place, which we won't be finding ahead of here."

They left the three mules hobbled and pushed ahead, Micky Free still leading the pack mule— sometimes being led by it, since the mule seemed to find the increasingly precipitous paths easier going than the men did, especially now that they were laden with some of the supplies and equipment that their mounts had carried.

The sixth night found them pressed into niches in the rock, sitting upright, chilled to the bone; there was no place level enough to lie down. Sleep was impossible, but it was enough, Horn felt, not to be moving. He recalled, with some envy, lizards he had seen in the desert, active and lively when the sun hit them, and then just seeming to turn off, like a stopped steam engine, when it got cold. Right now, it seemed like a good way of doing things. It took a creature as damn foolish as a man to keep going when it was this cold.

In the middle of the next morning, their slow progress came to a halt. Sieber studied the maze of rock and underbrush ahead, then the precipitous dropoff to their left. Horn and Micky Free watched him silently.

After a while, Sieber shook his head. "I can't make out the way, can you?" Neither bothered to reply; it had not been a real question.

Horn watched as Sieber moved away from them, fiercely concentrating on the terrain. The scout moved among the rocks and brush, running his fingertips over the surface of a boulder, studying the leaves and their coloration, then brushing the rocks gently again. Horn could sense that he was tuning himself up, opening up so that the country itself could speak to him and let him know its secrets. Horn wondered what in hell Sieber's bright eyes might be casting about for . . . then knew he had found it, whatever it was, as he stiffened, hurried back to them, and pointed off to the left.

"*That* way," he said. They looked in the direction he indicated, and Horn closed his eyes briefly, then opened them. He hadn't made any mistake; Sieber was pointing straight out over the dropoff.

He joined the scout and moved to view it. It was an almost vertical rock face, ending fifteen feet or more down in a tumble of rocks and scree. A man could make the jump and maybe not be hurt, but a mule would be lucky to break only a leg or so. But Sieber was calling the shots, and if he said that was the way, that was the way. There sure didn't seem to be any other.

The unburdened mule was left to wander back down to the plains if it could make it, or to run wild in the mountains; Horn figured it would probably have an easier time of it either way than he and his companions would. He and Micky Free dropped the supplies the mule had been carrying down the rock face, cushioning some of them in blanket wrappings. Micky Free seemed amused at the heavy thudding sound the bundles made hitting the rock below; Horn did not see anything funny about it.

With their gear dropped, Horn was the first to follow it. He lowered himself over the edge, craned his head awkwardly downward to try to find the best—or the least unpromising, at any rate—landing spot, and pushed off, aiming for it. He hit hard, giving at the knees, and rolled onto his back, following through in a motion that brought him to his feet. He stood, slightly winded but unhurt, and watched Micky Free's clumsier landing, from which the little half-breed emerged with a broad smile and an upward glance—as if, Horn thought, it had been such fun that he had half a mind to find a way back up and do it all over again.

Sieber's fall was awkward and hard, his bad leg hitting ground first and driving a gusty breath—not really a groan—from him. He sat for a moment, fiercely kneading the leg, then looked up at Horn standing above him. "It hurts," he said, apparently feeling that his action needed some explanation.

"It figured," Horn said. "You going to be okay?"

Sieber got to his feet slowly. "Going to hurt if I go on or if I don't," he muttered. "You got something like this, it don't matter much what you do, it'll go on hurting, so you might as well do what you got to do."

They left at least half the supplies behind, but the remainder, distributed among them and loaded on their backs, more than doubled the awkwardness and effort of their progress. Horn, skidding on loose rock, almost pitched over a cliff; Micky Free, putting a foot wrong, slid twenty feet down a slope, stopping himself only by grabbing a gnarled tree stump, around which he swung himself a couple of times, clearly enjoying it immensely. Sieber, Horn noted, though pained by his leg, picked his way as sure-footedly as a mountain goat.

That night, they did not sleep or rest; at Sieber's urging, they kept on. "I can tell it," he had said, staring ahead in the dusk at the mountains which looked to Horn about like all the others they had seen, "we are just about there. That rounded peak there, like a lady's tit, and that saddle off to the right, I know them. We ain't got much further to go, and the place we're going to, I think it's a good thing we get there in the dark."

Hours later, after a nightmare of stumbling and crawling over invisible pathways, Horn agreed. Prone and peering through a screen of bushes into a hollow, he could see only the fitful blaze of several small fires and the wavering shadows of those who moved among them; but knowing that those shadows were cast by Geronimo's picked warriors made him grateful for the shelter of night.

"How'd you know about this place?" Horn whispered.

"Didn't," Sieber said with a shrug Horn could barely make out. "But me and Geronimo, we go back twenty years. He used to like this spot as a main base—figured the cavalry might have a little trouble charging in at him." The distant firelight glinted off

Sieber's teeth as he exposed them in a brief smile. "He didn't get where he got by being dumb."

They stared at the fires until they guttered down to embers, studding the dark with dimmed brightness, no longer casting shadows. If any of Geronimo's men were patrolling their camp this late, their fires did not betray them.

The sun had cleared the peaks to the east and was flooding the hollow. What it illuminated would have surprised the town-dwelling folk who prized chromolithographs of scenes of life among the noble red men. The Apaches did not go in for the glorious buffalo-hide tipis of the Sioux or the sod-covered hogans of the Navaho. Even in this bitter weather, they found that a tangle of small branches supported by a larger one punched into the rocky ground sufficed to provide shelter from the wind and snow, with heat provided by tiny fires in the center of each untidy structure around which the inhabitants could curl their bodies. To Horn's eye, Geronimo's village looked like a patch of brushwood someone had cut over and made a poor try at tidying up. A few old women and small children moved about it, intent on whatever it was Apache women and children did in the absence of the warriors.

"The men been gone over an hour," he said.

Sieber nodded, then rose to his feet, motioning Horn and Micky Free to do the same. They had worked their way to within thirty yards of the village under cover of the brush and rocks, and had watched the departure of Geronimo and his fighting horde just after dawn. Horn had figured that it would be an easy enough shot to kill Geronimo from ambush and wind up the whole business, but Sieber had negated the idea in a violent whisper. "Geronimo is important because he's a better fighter than a hundred-fifty Lawtons or so, even if you steam-distill them and get rid of all the shit—but the real reason he's important is that the Apache will do what he tells them. Without him, all the braves will just go on fighting because they don't know anything else to do—not so good as they would with him leading them, but good enough so nobody's hair is going to be safe in the Southwest for fifty years, and I don't think General Crook or President Cleveland is going to be happy to wait till 1936 before they can say the West is pacified. What we got to do is make it so Geronimo does our work for us."

Now, with the early sun on them, festooned with ammunition belts, each with a rifle in one hand and a pistol in the other, they advanced on the camp, Horn and Sieber grim and tense, Micky Free wolfishly happy.

They covered half the distance before one old woman, bent over a battered gallon can apparently serving as a cookpot, looked up and saw them. She spoke to the crones gathered near her, who turned to stare at the oncoming white men.

Then they were within the beaten-earth perimeter of the Indian village—or camp, or dump, you could call it any of those, Horn thought. The women and children had silently drifted together; dark eyes in dark faces regarded them without visible emotion.

Sieber halted and turned to Micky Free. "Do it." He flung Horn, Micky Free, and the huddled Apaches a look that seemed to contain a full load of rage, disgust, and resignation, then waved his hand in a gesture that took in the whole camp. "All of it . . . all yours."

Micky Free, fumbling at his belt, took off at a run for the center of the shabby village.

"I hate this," Sieber muttered. "My home was taken . . . the old country . . . I was little only, but still I remember . . ."

Flame blossomed in Micky Free's hand as he ran; he whirled the lit torch above his head in a circle.

"The French hate the Germans," Sieber mused. "The Germans hate the English, the English hate the French . . . Micky is Apache but he hates Geronimo because Micky is Tonto Apache and Geronimo is Chiricahua Apache. . . ."

Micky Free dipped his torch to a stick shelter; it flamed instantly. He ran to the next, and the next.

Sieber watched him gloomily. "Hate is a lot of shit."

"Then why are you doing all this?" Horn asked.

"I got to punish Geronimo—better he surrender to Crook than Miles. Crook will treat him fair."

"Why does he have to surrender at all? This—" Horn gestured at the mountain vista that stretched away around them. "—this is *his* old country."

Sieber looked at Horn dully. Good question, young Horn, he thought. The *why* of anything had never bothered Sieber much, not even in the War—that, and then the twenty years of scouting and learning the West, they had been something to be done, and he had done it, liking some of it, hating some of it—but, times, now, with the gray spreading in his hair and beard and his body slowing down, the *whys* would come to him in the night when he couldn't sleep. Because he needed the sleep, he would push them away and make himself think of something else. And now, having done that for so long, he had no answer. . . . He blinked and shook his head. "I don't know."

He followed Horn's gaze to where Micky Free was torching the remaining shelters, and gestured toward the huddle of old women. "Tell them we're sorry."

Horn gave him a sardonic look, stepped toward the women, and spoke to them in Apache. He blinked in surprise when what looked to be the oldest of them, a mummy-like woman who could have been a hundred, croaked a reply in English. "Tell Sibi . . . no one smiles."

The last of the shelters was aflame now; the first ones to be ignited were heaps of embers, with white ash already beginning to form on them.

In the misty dawn, Horn could see the Sierra Madres rising above the scouts' camp. It felt damned good to be out of them, back on comparatively level ground again. Comparatively only; the shallow natural bowl Crawford had picked was strewn with boulders, many of them half again the height of a man. He had, he considered, had about enough of mountains, where every step you took, practically, had to be up or down. The last stage of the journey had been mostly down—himself, Sieber, and Micky Free, and the captive Apaches, sometimes sliding down slopes, sometimes having to be lowered over a cliff on ropes. It was quicker going than Sieber's circuitous approach to Geronimo's camp had been, but definitely a one-way route. Horn had been wary of a stab from a concealed knife wielded by one of the women, or even the children, but Sieber had reassured them. "Now we burned their village and took their stuff, they got to stick with us, they know when we get them down to Crawford and the rest, they get fed and took care of. Up here, with the men away, they starve and freeze in a couple days. Apaches is practical people, some ways; they like to stay alive so that maybe someday they get to see Geronimo bring you or me in for them to go to work on—Apache women can think up lots of things to do to prisoners."

Horn had been impressed by the stoic toughness with which the prisoners, even the oldest of the old women, had stood the ordeal of the descent to the plains. There had been one bad place, where the ancient woman had had to be bundled in a blanket tied to a rope, and let down for nearly thirty feet; but she hadn't yelled or complained. He saw her now, in the morning mists, talking with some of the other women and the old men, the ones Crawford and the scouts had picked up in their sweep.

One very old man detached himself from the group and spoke to Horn in Apache. Horn replied respectfully, trotted to the supply tent, and returned with some food, which he handed over. The old man gave him a brief acknowledgment, devoid of gratitude, and moved away.

Lieutenant Lawton had observed the exchange and frowned as Horn came toward him. "It's not good to let them order you around like that."

Horn gave him a disgusted look. "That was *Nana*, for chrissakes."

Lawton was, in spite of himself, impressed. Nana's

day was past, but in it he had been as fearsome a figure in the Indian wars as Geronimo. And he, Henry Lawton, had had a hand in taking him in . . . it was irritating that he had had to be told the identity of his captive by a scruffy civilian, but no matter. . . . That might make a good passage in a book, if he ever got to writing one, the way Custer had. Of course, Custer had been unlucky in his choice of a title: after Little Big Horn, *My Experiences With Indians* had a taint of macabre humor. . . .

"How do you know so much about Apaches?" he asked.

"Lived with 'em," Horn said, and gave him a long, level look. "How do *you* know so little?"

He moved away from the lieutenant and toward the Indians. The oldest woman, the one who had addressed him in English back in Geronimo's camp, came over to him and began speaking in Apache. "There is food, as you promised," she said, "but it has no taste. It would be a good thing if some of the younger women were let out to gather some herbs to flavor it."

Horn grinned. Such a herb-gathering party, he was pretty sure, would return late in the day and shy one woman—who would by then be hotfooting it to let Geronimo know what had happened and where his captive people were. "That would be a good thing," he said. "It would be a better thing if the women stayed here, where nothing bad could happen to them."

The old woman gave him a sour smile and a nod, admitting defeat. She might have had the last word in the brief conversation, and was opening her mouth for it when Horn heard a far-off popping noise and, close by, the sharp yet muffled sound of a bullet striking flesh; the old woman spun away backward, bright blood spraying from her mouth.

CHAPTER 8

Horn dove and caught her before she hit the ground; then, seeing she was dead, let go of her and flattened himself against the rocky ground.

There were more popping sounds coming out of the mist. No visible source: whoever it was must be firing pretty nearly blindly—not entirely, Horn realized, for the shots were finding targets; Indians, scouts, and captives alike were falling, and screams of pain and fear mingled with the sound of the guns. He gauged the distance to the nearest rocks that were sizable enough to provide shelter from the firing, came up from the ground to a crouch, and ran for the rocks.

A slug hit the largest boulder just as he reached it, and caromed off with a spiteful whine, its impact sending stinging rock dust into his eyes; he blinked against the pain, scrambled over the rock, and dropped behind it. Sieber, Crawford, and Lawton were there before him, flattened against the boulder's side. Sieber and Crawford looked worried, Lawton, stunned. Not scared, Horn decided, Lawton wasn't that kind—maybe not bright enough, which was what passed for bravery a lot of times—but faced with something he hadn't expected and not up to it.

Crawford registered Horn's arrival without greeting him and said to Sieber, "Geronimo?"

Sieber shook his head. "Feels wrong."

Horn clambered up the rock and peered over its edge. The mist was thinner now, and he could see dim shapes, a hundred yards or more off, across a flat space of rocky ground. Muzzle flashes winked against the gray background . . . and so did something else, more faintly—glints of reflected diffuse sunlight on metal fittings. . . . Now he could make out tall hats on the gradually more visible enemy.

"It's Mexicans!" he called out, dropping down behind the boulder as the firing increased, sending what sounded like a flight of hornets snapping past his head. "Maybe fifty or so, what I could make out. What the *hell* . . . ?"

Sieber scowled in bafflement, then nodded his head. "I bet they think we're Indians."

"We *are* Indians," Horn said, "except for us."

"They get paid for every dead hostile," Sieber explained. "They must think that's what we all are. I got to get Emmet to try and stop this."

He turned to confer with Crawford. Horn eased his head around the side of the rock for another look at the scene of battle. The captive Apaches were huddled quietly together behind some low rocks, shielding their dead. The scouts—except for four who lay unmoving and bloody in the dust—were out of sight but not out of hearing; from behind anything that would serve as shelter, they were sending a deafening barrage of return fire. Now Horn could hear an occasional scream from the Mexicans and see explosive puffs of dust as the scouts' bullets struck into their line.

He half expected a return of the dreamlike state that had possessed him in the fight at Cibucu, but it did not come. All the same, he was interested to note, he was not particularly scared. It was not what he would choose, having fifty or whatever Mexicans trying to shoot his ass off, but that was what was happening, and the main thing was to work out what to do about it.

"Handkerchief," Crawford said. Horn blinked at him and pulled a red- and blue-patterned bandana from his rear trousers pocket. Crawford shook his head. "White." He turned to Lawton, who pulled a square of snowy cloth from the cuff of his left sleeve— the spit-and-polish way of doing things came in handy sometimes, Horn reflected.

Crawford tied the handkerchief to a stick, poked it over the top of the rock, and waved it back and forth. It had no apparent effect on the Mexican troops; the volume of their gunfire remained undiminished.

"Cease firing," Crawford called to Horn. Horn relayed the command in Apache to the hidden scouts, who responded, if at all, by shooting even more rapidly. Horn repeated the order in a throat-wrenching yell, embellishing it with some unmilitary but pungent comments about the penalties of disobedience; the scouts' fire slackened, then died away.

After another volley, the Mexican troops also let their guns fall silent. Now the only sounds were human, squeezed from the wounded by their pain and despair.

Horn looked at Crawford. After a moment the cap-

tain nodded. Horn moved from behind the safety of
the rock; Crawford, holding the improvised flag of
truce high and waving it, followed him.

The sun had burned the mist away by now, and
Horn could see the Mexican troops clearly; and, even
more vividly, the stretch of open ground between the
two sides. Each of the scattered rocks or sparse
patches of sage seemed to have its own individual
identity; and any one of them, Horn was uncomfortably aware, might mark the place where he would die.

Crawford, next to him, was sweating profusely,
though the day was not yet really warm. The captain's
face was pale, and the arm with which he was waving
the flag trembled, adding a flutter to its motion. Horn
had seen him, earlier in the morning, taking a quick
pull at his flask, and wondered if the jolt of whiskey
was making it easier or harder for Crawford to do
what he was doing. The man beside him didn't seem
much like the fighting bull of Sieber's reminiscences;
but there was enough of him left to do what he had to
do.

He could see the Mexican troops more clearly now:
a rank in front, prone, another behind them, kneeling,
all with rifles pointed squarely at him and Crawford.
The rifles got larger with each step he took, a little
larger and a lot uglier. He did not turn, but knew that
twenty-some rifles were aimed in their general direction from behind them. If any kind of balloon went
up, there would be an almighty cross fire, right where
he and Crawford were walking. . . . Behind the
troops, four men—officers, by their trappings and the
fact that they held pistols, not rifles—stood watching
intently. Off to the left, a jacketless Mexican soldier,

his shirt sleeves rolled up, was bent over one of a row of men lying on the ground; there was blood on his shirtfront, and cries—strangely muted, it seemed to Horn, who then realized that some part of his mind was filtering out whatever it didn't need to deal with the immediate situation—came from the wounded men the soldier was trying to tend. Four or five men, made shapeless by the blankets that covered them from face to foot, lay a little farther off. There's enough of 'em down so they're hurting, Horn thought. Bad enough to make 'em ready to talk truce, or just killing mad . . . ?

They were halfway toward the Mexican line now. Horn stopped and looked to Crawford for instructions. The captain's eyes were closed and his mouth slightly open as he breathed hoarsely; he swayed as he stood. His training, or what remained of his spirit, had got him this far, Horn saw, but that was about it for Crawford. He wondered, with a flash of irritation, what made a man keep on in a trade that was likely to land him in situations like this when he wasn't up to it anymore; it made for doing things in a half-assed way. Two goddamn West Pointers in charge of this outfit, and yet it had been sneaked up on by a bunch of troops with no warning. . . .

He turned toward the Mexicans and shouted in Spanish. After a moment an answering call came from the officer with the most brass and silver glinting on his uniform.

"What'd you tell 'em?" Crawford muttered.

"That we were sent by the government to bring back Geronimo." Horn cut his eyes over to Crawford. With something actually happening, the captain seemed to be pulling himself together.

The Mexican commander conferred with his officers, then shouted again to Horn.

"He wants to know why so many Indians," Horn said.

Crawford gave him a tight grin. "Tell him General Crook says it takes one to catch one."

Horn relayed the reply to the Mexicans. The officers consulted again. Horn could see their heads nodding and thought he caught the hint of a smile, though it was hard to be sure at that distance. Then the commander gave them a broad wave of his uplifted hand.

Horn saw Crawford relax, almost sagging into a slouch. "By God, we did it," he said. Horn nodded, feeling the tension seep out of his body. Now that it was over, he could let himself realize just how scared he had been. Crawford lowered the flag, and they both turned toward the scouts' camp. Horn could see Sieber, leaning on the rock and lowering his rifle to rest against it.

As they walked toward the camp, Horn noted that his shoulders were twitching in a sort of shudder, as if his body, denied the release of trembling during the crisis, were, independent of his will or awareness, making up for that denial.

His right arm swung out in front of him, hit in its upper part by what felt like a sledge, and blood sprayed in the air. He stumbled and was down before he was aware of hearing the shot that had caught him, and the ones that followed.

He scrabbled at the stony ground and pushed himself to his feet. He took a lurching step and cursed as the dangling arm sent a jolting stab of pain through him, then grabbed it with his left hand and ran, crouching. Without the use of his arms, his balance was disastrously thrown off, but he pounded awkwardly ahead, compensating as best he could. Dust clouds erupted beside and ahead of him as the Mexican bullets sought but did not find him. The trancelike sureness that had infused him in Cibucu Canyon, even the conscious quelling of fear of the walk toward the Mexican lines, was gone now—he was a wounded, panicked animal, running from sure death, only enough of the reasoning human left to him to realize that the odds of making it were dreadfully slim . . . and to despise the naked fear that drove him.

Then he was behind the sheltering rock in the camp, Sieber beside him, looking down at him. He panted like a dog and clutched his arm. Sieber was the iron man; Sieber would help him. . . .

"Christ," Sieber said, almost moaning it. He pointed out over the bare stretch of land between them and the still-firing Mexicans. Horn hitched himself to the edge of the rock and looked out. His mind was starting to work again, and he noted and relished the storm of gunfire coming from the scouts scattered around the camp; they were fewer than the Mexes but using their weapons more effectively.

Then he saw a limp shape in the dust, halfway toward the enemy. Polished boots, blue uniform trousers tucked into them, red stains turning the blue jacket to purple, bright red covering the head. He realized that he couldn't remember if Crawford was—had been—blond or brown-haired, and there was sure-God no way of telling now. Then the figure moved. Its hands clawed at the blood-soaked dust around it, the legs thrashed, and it was somehow lifting itself away from the ground, shuddering as another bullet slammed into it, but keeping moving anyway.

"Christ," Sieber repeated, very softly. "He's still alive."

The bloodied figure pulled its legs and arms close enough to its trunk to permit it to hitch itself along on the dusty, reddening ground. It moved erratically, with no evident goal, changing direction as bullets slammed into it.

"*Christ!*" Horn yelled, and took off at a run from behind the rock, ignoring the pain from his wounded arm, making it work to keep his balance in spite of its protests. He had no thought of why he was doing this, or even what it was he was doing. The existence of the twitching, mindless figure on the ground could have no other result than to send him toward it, weaving and bobbing to avoid the enemy's aim. There was no more decision about it than there was about a bullet's plans for traveling down the rifle barrel when the powder charge explodes.

Behind him, Sieber lifted his rifle and fired again and again into the Mexican line. The Indian scouts shifted their fire to the area of the line that seemed to pose the most danger to Horn, and somehow managed to increase their volume until it was a steady roar. Goddam Gettysburg all over again, Sieber thought, with a grim relish. We poured it into them Secesh, and they broke—if we'd had some of my scouts there, they'd of broke sooner, I bet.

Among the huddled captives, old Nana straightened, ran to where a scout lay dead, scooped up his rifle and ammunition, and scrambled up to the top of a boulder. His ninety-year-old eyes could not see the details of the weapon very clearly—he relied on practiced fingers to slip the loads into the firing chamber—but for distance, they were sharper than when he had been in his prime. Every detail of the Mexican line was brilliantly clear to him. He smiled briefly, picked his target, squeezed off the shot, and saw the kneeling soldier spin out of the line, sprawling. He sniffed the dusty, warm air, with its scent of blood and powder, listened to the yells and screams and the sleeting rattle of gunfire. It was a good fight, this. And the crazy white man was making it even more interesting, running out like that to where the dying officer was. He would get honor for that, Nana thought; and that was interesting, too, since the Talking Boy was not like a young brave, anxious to make a name for himself. No person could ever really understand the white men. He fired again.

Horn, nearing Crawford, saw the captain rise to his knees, half stand, then spin into the dust as another bullet took him in the shoulder. Horn was aware of a steady pouring of blood from his own right arm and hand.

Then he was up to Crawford, crouching by him, trying to lift him. The right arm would not obey him; there was no strength in it. "Shit!" he said bitterly. "Bastard!" He wasn't clear about whether he was referring to the arm or to the helpless Crawford. He hooked his left hand into Crawford's blood-soaked uniform collar and began to drag him along; the captain's head flopped limply and his boot toes gouged trails in the dust.

No way to dodge now, Horn thought dully. Straight

ahead, don't bother to try outguessing the bullets, because there's nothing can be done about them. We make it, we make it, if we don't we don't. Only thing to do, take a fix on that big rock and go for it. He was dimly aware of an immense volume of firing from the scouts' camp, and perhaps a falling off of that from the Mexicans; but the sounds were far away, and getting fainter.

The rocks of the camp were closer now, but not close enough; he could feel his strength—his life, he supposed—draining away through his arm. He squeezed what remained of his will and consciousness into a tiny ball and tried to locate it just behind his eyes where it could observe and send orders to his failing body.

Just about at the rocks now, and there was Sieber, moving out, coming toward him, moving strangely, as if he were a fish swimming under water, then beside him, helping with Crawford, it was all right to let go, let the ground come up and take him.

The low plateau a little under a quarter of a mile off afforded an excellent view of the battle, with the whole scene spread out like one of those shows the buffalo hunter put on, making a children's story out of the wars between the whites and the People. This was no children's story, though, but a good, sharp fight. The solitary man on horseback considered that the Mexicans had been foolish. The silent approach to the camp, and then the work with the knife until secrecy became impossible, and only then shooting, at close quarters where there was no chance to miss; that would have been the way to do it. But Mexicans always fired too soon.

He looked down at the pack of lean hounds that surrounded him, then back at the battle. There were many dead already; there would be many more. And—except for the Indian captives, in any case only old men, women, and children, no warriors—none of them any friends of his.

Geronimo smiled.

CHAPTER 9

A rag bound tightly around Horn's arm stopped the worst of the bleeding. A dash of whiskey from Crawford's flask, pulled from his sodden pocket, gave the wound a rough cleansing and shocked him into wakefulness; another measure of it sent warmth flooding through him as he gulped it down.

He went to Sieber, who was bent over Crawford. The captain was a patchwork of blood and dust; but his chest still moved and an irregular harsh rasping came from his throat. Sieber sponged at his face with a rag dipped in water.

Something about the sound of gunfire caught Horn's attention. He looked toward the Mexican line. The soldiers seemed farther away; and as he watched, he saw the remnants of the front rank scramble to their feet and move back some ten yards before reforming and firing again. The other rank executed the same maneuver; and in a few moments the entire detachment was out of effective rifle range. The scouts' fire became sporadic, confined to a few ambitious marksmen trying for a really challenging shot.

Lieutenant Lawton, looking white and worried, came up to where Sieber was tending Crawford; so did Nana, who squatted beside the wounded man. Sieber spoke briefly with him, handed over the rag with which he had been sponging Crawford's face, and stood up. Maybe, Horn thought, old Nana had some Indian medicine tricks that would do Crawford some good. It surely didn't seem as if anything else they had on hand was going to help him.

"Still alive?" Horn said as Sieber approached him.

"Sort of." Sieber's face was drawn and old.

Horn heard shouts and turned. The Indian scouts were yelling at him to look toward the Mexicans again. He did, and grunted. "Now *they're* waving a white flag."

The Mexican officer holding the flag, and those around him, called to Horn in Spanish. Sieber looked at him, eyebrows raised. Horn grimaced and tightened the cloth around his arm—fresh blood was seeping through and trickling down his fingers. "They're sorry, they surrender. Can we try and help with their wounded?" His voice was flat with anger, contempt, and the dregs of the fear and pain that had filled him.

"Can we?" Sieber said.

Horn looked at him. "I'm not in charge, Mr. Sieber."

Sieber peered toward the Mexican lines. There was hardly a shrub or clump of grass left standing where their first position had been, and it was marked by a rubbishy litter of broken and abandoned equipment and a scatter of irregular dark stains. Where they were now, there seemed to be more of them down, many shrouded in blankets, than on their feet; thin cries of pain drifted steadily to him over the distance between them. He sighed gustily and said, "I'll go check how bad they are."

He took a stride toward the edge of the camp, then stopped and peered sharply to the south. "Look." He pointed. "It's *him*."

Horn squinted. He could see against the skyline the rock-still mounted man. The commanding immobility of the remote figure might have been enough of a clue, but the lean, restless shapes clustered about the horse made it certain. "Always with those dogs," he muttered.

Sieber nodded and began moving toward the Mexican lines. Horn squinted and, for a long time, looked across the heated, shimmering air at Geronimo.

Ten minutes later, Horn was seated in the shadow of the large rock, working on the binding up of his arm. It hurt but wasn't bleeding anymore; thank God the bullet had gone through and wouldn't have to be dug out. He saw Nana still trying to do something for Crawford, a little distance away, while Lawton watched nervously. Sonofabitch is just realizing he's about got a battlefield promotion, Horn thought, and he don't know shit what to do about it.

"Mr. Horn!" Sieber's bellow was thinned by the distance.

Horn turned toward the Mexican lines, out of sight from where he sat. "I hear you."

"They would like mules to carry their wounded."

I bet they would. "How many?"

"All."

Horn grinned and shook his head. "Tell 'em to go to hell. Word you want is *infierno*."

"I would like very much to do that," Sieber called. "Except that they will kill me."

75

Horn leaped at the side of the rock, grabbing for holds with his left hand, his rifle held awkwardly in the crook of his right elbow, and scrambled to the top. He saw Sieber in the center of a ring of Mexican soldiers, each with a rifle trained on him. "It seems I am held captive."

Horn slammed his left fist on the rock and swore. He heard running footsteps below him and looked down to see Lawton staring agitatedly up at him. "We can't give 'em our mules," the lieutenant said urgently. "We're two hundred miles from the border, and I'm not walking out of Mexico!"

Horn hardly heard him. He was seeing the moves that could be made, that had to be made, as clearly as if they were drawn out on the rock before him. He cupped his hands and shouted in Spanish. The Mexican commander called a reply.

Lawton looked at him anxiously. "What was that you just said?"

"That we had forty mules and to send a dozen men to get 'em."

Lawton glared and jutted his jaw. "You *remember* something, mister—Crawford's done and I'm in command and you by God rescind what you just did!"

"*You* remember something." Horn's voice was almost a whisper, leaded with venom. "Everybody hates you here." His left hand snaked the rifle from its resting place and brought it to bear on the lieutenant. "Give me trouble, I'll blow your *head* into the rocks. It'll be an accident, and every scout here will say the same thing—'Poor Henry Lawton, the Mexicans shot him while he was running away.'"

Lawton looked into the rifle barrel for a moment,

then turned sharply and stamped across the ground to where Crawford lay.

Horn slid down from the rock, and called orders to the scouts. In a few minutes the forty mules were gathered into a group in the center of the camp, with a handful of the scouts in charge. A party of a dozen Mexicans, officers and men, left their line and approached the camp.

Horn watched, saw their slow advance until they were lost from his sight in the jumble of upright rocks at the camp's perimeter, then made a sign to the remainder of the scouts.

Sieber, sweating in the sun, yet feeling an almost palpable chill coming to him from the rifle barrels that ringed him, grinned as he looked across to the camp. The dozen Mexicans were in view again, hands high and moving agitatedly . . . under the guns of the Apache scouts.

There was a rapid-fire burst of Spanish between Horn and the Mexican commander; then Horn called to Sieber, "I told him I'd trade his twelve for you. He asked how he could trust me to release his men if he releases you first."

Sieber's tongue seemed to stick to the dry roof of his mouth, but he managed to call, "What did you say?"

"I said . . ." Horn's voice came across the space between them, "he *couldn't* trust me."

Sieber could see him, turning and barking a guttural command in Apache to the scouts surrounding the dozen Mexicans; then the click of weapons being cocked came to him.

A protesting babble of Spanish arose from the captives. Horn grinned, then called across to Sieber, "The Indians start firing in fifty seconds." He turned to the Mexicans, and said, smiling broadly, "*Cinquenta secundos.*" The ringing Apache scouts looked hungrily at the Mexicans.

Sieber took in the picture and glanced again at the rifles pointed at his head. "I'm too old for this kind of thing, Mr. Horn."

Horn called back, "It'll all be over soon." He paused and added, "One way or the other." To the Mexicans in his charge, he said, "*Cuarenta secundos.*" He could see that one of the soldiers had his eyes closed and was moving his lips rhythmically, and wondered if he was praying or counting off seconds.

"*Treinta,*" Horn told the Mexicans. He spoke to his scouts in Apache; they slowly raised their rifles and pointed them at the soldiers.

"*Veinte.*"

Sieber closed his eyes, the sweat pouring off his face, and wondered just how much it was going to hurt.

The Mexican commander stared wildly at the hostage scout, and at the twelve men of his command—after the fight, a substantial percentage of his ablebodied troops—who stood under the guns of the Apaches, gesticulating and calling, pleading, to him. He saw the mad American with the rag around his arm, the one who had somehow lived through the rain of fire his men had poured out, raise one hand and spread the fingers twice, signing that the dozen soldiers there now had ten seconds to live. An eerie chanting arose from the Indians around them; the commander had heard that chant in Apache camps and recalled very clearly what captured soldiers had looked like after it had been sung. His men were screaming now. . . .

He cursed and shoved Sieber stumbling away from the rifles pointed at him. "*Vaya!*" he spat. "*Vaya.*"

Sieber stood for a second, then began walking across the open stretch between the Mexicans' position and the camp. He could see the stained ground, a little ahead, where Crawford had been shot under the flag of truce, and his back twinged in fear and anticipation. He wanted desperately to break into a run, but forced himself to hobble along slowly. Sweat poured down his face, and his clothes stuck to him as if he had been in a rainstorm.

Horn squinted across to the Mexican lines, holding his rifle left-handed, anchored against his side. No good for accurate shooting, but, if it came to it, he could throw some lead that way, and there were still plenty of targets.

Sieber heard from behind him the sound of a rifle being cocked, and altered in his stride, but kept on. From ahead came Horn's shout: "Don't even *think* about it!"

The Mexican officer with the raised rifle glared across at the scouts' camp, fought with his anger and humiliation for an instant, then lowered his weapon.

Sieber stumbled the last few steps into camp. Horn came to meet him, paying no attention to the fresh seeping of blood from his wound. "You okay?"

"Why shouldn't I be okay?" Sieber said gruffly. But the hand he extended to greet Horn was trembling violently.

Horn led him to rest in the shade, then went to see

to the return of the dozen Mexicans. To Lawton's consternation, he insisted on sending back four mules with them.

"Damn it, mister, you're just rewarding treachery!"

Horn shrugged. "With the mules for their wounded, they can move away from here faster, get back to their base and make a report, get the wounded tended to. With no mules, most of the hurt men'll die by the time they get back, and the commander'll be shamed, have to resign or shoot himself or something honorable like that. He's got nothing to lose, so he'd be dogging us all the way to the border, waiting for a good place for an ambush and another try at the mules. Anyhow, we can spare 'em. Used up half our supplies already, shot off about a mule load of ammunition this morning."

Lawton seemed to be trying to riffle through an invisible manual, looking for a passage that covered the situation. "Damn it, I don't like this."

Sieber, a little rested, hobbled over to them. "You don't have to like it, Lieutenant, so long as you do it. You got to give these fellows enough to let them live, or they be at us forever. You want to be all military and proper and keep all your mules, there's one way, of course."

"What's that?" Lawton said.

"I turn my scouts loose at nightfall, tell them to have some fun. Come morning, we got a barrelful of Mexican scalps, and nobody going back to Chihuahua to make reports about us. But I don't think you got the stomach for that."

Lawton shuddered. "All right. Four mules. But not the best ones."

In an hour, the Mexican detachment had moved off and was nearly out of sight, a cloud of dust on the plain dwindling against the backdrop of the snow-topped mountains.

The dead—four of the captive Indians, including the old woman who had been the first casualty, and five scouts—were buried under the direction of Nana, whose cracked voice intoned the death chant.

The scouts dug, a little to one side of the others, a tenth grave. It would be needed soon. . . .

Horn was sitting, working on a final bandage for his arm, when Sieber came to him from where Crawford lay. Horn looked up and Sieber nodded his head slowly, looking almost on the point of tears. "I . . . I wanted to thank you for what you did for Emmet," he said huskily.

"I didn't do anything for Emmet," Horn said. "He died."

Anger hardened the grief out of Sieber's face as he looked down at Horn. "You can *irritate* people, Mr. Horn, you know that?" he said loudly. "I'm angry as hell right now—and you just saved my life!"

Horn looked at him with interest. "What're you mad about?"

"Because it was all so goddam easy—you didn't even *sweat* much."

Horn considered this. It hadn't felt easy; but then again, it hadn't felt particularly hard, even when it had been all he could do to keep going. Right then, it had just been doing what had to be done, and how it felt wasn't that important. He resumed work on his bandage, and said, "I got shot, didn't I?"

"Did it *hurt?*" Sieber said hotly. "You didn't show."

Horn could not quite understand what Sieber was driving at. You get a bullet through your arm, tearing up flesh and muscle, of course it's going to hurt; nobody would shoot you unless it was going to hurt you or kill you. But there was no percentage in jumping up and down and hollering, "Look, everybody! I been shot!" He looked up at Sieber and said, "I do the best I can, that's all."

"You don't do best, you do better," Sieber said. "People are not *grateful* because you're better—you win too much and too easy and it don't cost you nothing."

Horn, losing interest in the discussion, said, "I'm just trying to make it through the day."

Sieber gritted his teeth and glared at him. "Well, don't expect gratitude from the masses, Mr. Horn. No one's gonna thank you, they're only gonna screw you if they can, they're gonna bring you *down!*"

Horn paid no attention. The bandage was just about right now, the ends of the cloth, neatly knotted, drawing it together firmly but not too tightly. The knots could be slipped easily for changing the dressing, then retightened. There was one ragged edge dangling which spoiled the look of the thing; he trimmed it awkwardly but carefully with his knife, then looked at it with satisfaction. It was done right, now, just the way it should be.

CHAPTER 10

A scatter of small cook fires broke the darkness. Sieber and Horn sat near the edge of the camp, well away from the others, as they ate. Horn could see the solitary figure of Lawton at his own fire; the lieutenant had seemed prepared to stifle his dislike of Horn and condescend to join them, but Sieber's icy stare had discouraged him.

A sharp sound came from the night, then another. "Dogs," Sieber muttered. A current of darkness, not as palpable as a wind, seemed to sweep across the camp, as the shadowy figures around the fires stiffened, then relaxed in reaction to the distant barking.

Now it was closer. Horn stood and helped Sieber to his feet. They moved away from the fires. The barking was louder and closer now; then, the dogs still invisible, it was all around them, and the hot, rank smell of the animals was in their nostrils.

"Sibi." The voice from the darkness was deep and resonant. Horn had never heard it before, but could sense the power, tenacity, and force of will of its owner, almost more clearly than if he could see him.

"Chief," Sieber said gravely. A rattle of Apache came in reply.

"He wants to know who I am," Horn said.

"Tell him you're the Talking Boy and you speak four languages."

Horn nodded and addressed the shadows, then listened attentively to the answer. "He'll surrender to Crook at Fort Bowie the first of next month."

Sieber glanced sardonically at Horn. "I wonder if he isn't just trying to get us to stop pressuring him. Ask him why not surrender now?"

After the next exchange with Geronimo, Horn said, "He needs time to bring in all the hostiles, not just the ancient and the women. It's over, he says. Crook wins."

"Why?"

Horn spoke a single word in Apache. His eyes, away from the firelight, were accustoming themselves to the darkness, and he could make out an area of deeper shadow that could be a man. The reply, when it came, was slow and in deep, sad tones.

"Because," Horn translated carefully to Sieber, "my people are weary . . . and our homes are gone . . . and I am old and sick of war."

Sieber grunted. "I, too, am old, and sick of bullshit."

Horn started to translate, then stopped and turned to Sieber. "You sure you want me to say that? Word for word?"

Sieber nodded grimly. Horn spoke in Apache, rather less briskly than he had before.

For a moment there was dead silence. Horn watched the shadow closely for any sign of movement, say a rifle being brought up or a war club coming into position for a throw.

A rumble of full-throated laughter came from the

shadow, then died. As Horn began to relax, it was followed by a high-pitched whistle. At the signal, a huge
horse pounded at them out of the darkness; Horn and
Sieber scrambled out of its way as it passed them and
the shadow they had been addressing leaped onto its
back. In an instant, both had vanished in a diminish-
ing rattle of hoofbeats and the chorus of the following
hounds.

Just when all was silent again, they heard the keening cry of a hawk, and then another. They both knew
that hawks do not hunt at night, and were eerily
aware of the faceless host of unseen watchers that the
darkness might hold.

Without saying anything, they turned and made
their way back toward the flickering fires of the
camp.

Sieber looked at Horn as they walked. "You know,
after all these years . . . he still scares me."

He seemed to be waiting for Horn to admit a simi-
lar fear; but Horn did not reply.

Three weeks later, and two hundred and fifty miles
north, Horn sat his standing horse comfortably. It had
taken a while to get the hang of it, but riding with his
arm in a sling now came naturally to him. Mounting
and dismounting were the tricky parts, but he had
mastered that, too.

Sieber and Lawton and three other officers waited
with him, just behind General Crook. It tickled Horn
that, at even this crucial moment, Crook didn't bother
with a military appearance. The canvas suit he wore
today was even floppier than the one Horn had first
seen him in, and the broad-brimmed hat was getting

as scraggly around the edges as the untrimmed beard. Lawton, on the other hand, was all polished, shaved, gleaming, and clean, his uniform pressed to a smoothness close to that of cast iron. Some sergeant's wife, Horn guessed, had probably earned a fast two bits washing and pressing it for a couple of hours.

Sieber stiffened and pointed ahead. "He comes."

"Thank God," Crook said softly.

Horn saw a dust cloud in the distance. It gradually resolved into a number of Indians on horseback.

"I told Washington he was coming in," Crook muttered to Sieber. "And if he hadn't showed today, if he hadn't surrendered . . ." He shook his head, setting his hat brim quivering. "It would have been all over, at least for me."

They waited and watched as the dust cloud grew bigger. Horn wondered what Geronimo must feel like, giving up at last. If it was the only thing to do, then it was the only thing, but it wouldn't sit well with the old warrior. Trouble was, the poor bastard was in charge of all his people, and had to work out what was best for them. On his own, he'd have been free to pick and choose what suited him, and he'd have had a lot more choices. A mistake, Horn considered, to get yourself lumbered down that way.

Crook was evidently feeling the strain now. "Let's go hear what he has to say," he said, and sent his horse toward the approaching Indians. The others followed.

The dust was raised, Horn saw as they neared it, by livestock—cattle and sheep, even some pigs that darted squealing through the throng—as well as the Indians' mounts. He saw a child with a stick half again as tall as itself whacking a cow to keep it moving; then an old man on a horse, scarcely more than a limp bag of bones in the saddle; then a younger man, one bandaged arm bound tightly to his side and a glazed look in his eyes; then a giggling woman trying to keep her bunched skirt covering at least some of her as she straddled her horse. . . .

Sieber reined up as the motley swarm flowed around them, and stared wildly at Horn. "He didn't come!" he bawled.

Horn, the general, and the other officers looked around dazedly.

"He *was* only buying time!" Sieber called to Horn. "We were there after him, the Mexicans were after him—he double-crossed Crook . . ." The rest of what he was saying was lost in the noise of the passage of the Indians and their livestock.

"Louder," Horn called.

"I said Crook—Crook is finished—Crook is done!"

Horn looked toward the general. Crook was staring, stupefied, at the passing Indians, the old and the very young, the maimed and the useless, riding and walking past him on their way to a safe captivity, each one of them another nail in the coffin of his career.

The general rode out of the crowd and turned toward the distant fort. Horn, following, saw from the slump of his shoulders that Crook had read the situation as accurately as Sieber had.

It would be Miles, then, General Nelson A. Horn recalled Sieber's comment on him: "There is white peoples, there is colored peoples, there is assholes, and there is General Miles."

Well, Horn thought, I've worked for white people and colored people and assholes already, looks like I'm going to get to finish out the string. Damn, if that Geronimo isn't a cagey old bastard!

Horn, watching the defeated general ride back to his last command, was turning over in his mind what could be done about Geronimo; it would be something, wouldn't it, to bring him in, for real.

CHAPTER 11

Horn shifted uneasily from foot to foot. Sieber had insisted that they make a good appearance at this meeting—"General Miles is very big on appearances. He has twenty-five years in the Army, and learned only one thing, you look good, you get ahead—winning battles, losing, don't matter, you look good, you get the promotions"—and the new suit and starched shirt were chafing him. And he couldn't see that it had done much good. The crowd of big, fair-haired officers Miles had brought along to his new command made him look like a hard-bitten cow pony in a crowd of race horses, no matter what he was wearing. And Sieber looked like a dressed-up trained bear. Lawton, now, he was right at home in this crew, happy as a hog in clover, and had already maneuvered himself close to the general. Horn was glad that at least he and Sieber were toward the back of the large, freshly painted and tidied room in which the general was showing off his new toy.

He blinked as an intolerably bright light flashed across the room from the spidery mechanism set up by the window.

Miles, as large and floridly handsome as any of his

officers, though, Horn noticed, beginning to puff up a bit—maybe, he considered, emulating President Cleveland's physique; what would he do if the next President was a skinny little runt?—spoke with pride as he pointed to the machine.

"This is my heliograph, gentlemen. It's what's going to end the Indian terror and bring peace to Arizona." He pulled at a lever that swiveled the mirror mounted on the framework; a pinpoint of white light blossomed on a hillside that Horn knew to be five miles off.

"We live in an age of miracles," Sieber muttered to Horn. "Now assholes can talk to other assholes with mirrors."

Miles moved to a large map on the wall. "Each section of the map will have a heliograph and a troop detachment. Geronimo won't be able to make a move without our knowing it. When he tries to run, we'll just pass him on from section to section, fresh troops always available."

He glanced around with a tight smile, accepting the nods and murmurs of approval from his staff.

"I think we all agree," he continued, "that this will be best kept as a strictly military operation." He looked toward the back of the room where Sieber stood. "So discharge all scouts at once."

Sieber nodded. How the hell he was supposed to function as chief scout without any scouts to be chief of was beyond him, but probably prize-bull Miles would have some asshole military way to handle that.

"*All* scouts, without exception," Miles said with relish.

Sieber blinked. To Horn, beside him, it seemed al-

90

most as if he had been hit by a bullet. His face knotted, but he said nothing, and turned toward the door; Horn moved with him.

"Good-bye, Mr. Sieber," the general called.

"General Miles," Sieber muttered, pausing at the door.

"No comments about the heliograph?"

Sieber stopped and turned, a flush spreading on his seamed face. "You want a comment, I'll give you one. Glue."

Miles was taken aback. "Glue?"

"Uh-*huh*," Sieber said heavily. "That way, after you catch Geronimo with your funny mirrors, you can glue him down good so he don't try escaping."

Miles's face tightened, and he turned to his officers. "Let me get a bit more specific now as to the operation—"

Sieber cut in, losing the rein of control he had kept on his fury: "I'm not done with my *comment*, General. I been"—he stopped and breathed deeply—"twenty"—he stopped again, as if choking—"half my goddam *life* I spent trying to make things all right in Arizona and then one sentence from you and its all over."

He slammed his fist against his leg. "We known each other since Gettysburg, General, when you were a young officer and I got my leg shot up—I watched you then and the truth is, you were one dumb bastard." He reached for the door and stepped halfway through it. "You haven't got *no* smarter over the years."

Sieber strode from the room; Horn, following, took a backward look and saw that the general's face still bore its usual bland expression. There's a fellow wouldn't show it if he got shot, Horn thought, mainly because he wouldn't have the sense to know it.

Outside the building, Sieber was still in a rage. "In a few months they ask us back," he said bitterly. "They *beg* us back, you'll see. In the meantime"—he turned to Horn with a look of vindictive triumph—"*we'll* get rich!"

"Rich" and "ditch" rhyme, Horn thought, but that's about as close as they get. And both of them rhyme with "dumb.sonofabitch," which is what I have *got* to be for being here. Goddam arm's all healed up fine, just so's I can wear it out swinging this damn *pick*!

He grunted as he drove the pick into the hard ground and another chunk of it fell away, enlarging the long, curving ditch infinitesimally. His back ached from stooping, his arms ached from wielding the pick, his head ached from the blast of the sun; he was hot, soaked with sweat, caked with dirt, a lot of which seemed to have settled in his eyes, and felt that it would be nice to kill something or somebody, for any reason or no reason. It was no consolation that Sieber, stripped to the waist as Horn was, and flinging shovel loads of earth over the sides of the ditch, was no better off.

Horn cast a longing eye at the bottle of whiskey set on the shady side of the ditch—also a careful eye: there had been a tragedy last week when the sun had caught an unwatched bottle and heated it until the cork went flying like a bullet; the recoil had sent the bottle onto its side and most of its contents had foamed away into the dirt. He promised himself a drink after the next hundred strokes of the pick.

Counting would give him something to think about while he worked.

"I *hate* this," he called to Sieber.

Sieber flung another load out of the ditch. "It gets worse before it gets better."

"How do we know there's anything worth a goddam down there?" Horn asked.

"Because I am a great miner." Horn shot a look of scorn at him. "True," Sieber said pridefully. "I discovered the first copper mine in all Arizona. Last year alone, the profit was eight hundred thousand dollars."

Horn drove the pick with renewed enthusiasm. "Now I feel better." He raised the pick for another stroke, then paused. "Wait a minute. If you're so rich, what are you doing killing yourself? And me, come to that."

Sieber leaned on his shovel and studied its blade carefully. "I never said I was rich."

"You said . . ."

Sieber glared at him. "I did not say I still owned the mine."

"You sold it, you mean." Sieber nodded. "For how much?" Horn said tiredly.

"Too little," Sieber said.

"*How much?*"

Sieber's mumbled reply was approximately "Frundudulla," but Horn had no trouble at all in hearing it as "Four hundred dollars."

Horn said, "I just stopped feeling better," laid down his pick, grabbed the whiskey bottle, and took a long, long drink. He set the bottle down and gave Sieber a bitter look. "I hope we don't find anything—we can't afford it."

He lifted the pick and drove it into the earth viciously.

Light winked in the distance, a point of hot white against the hazy dun of a low hill. The corporal peered at the flickering signal and jotted on a pad supported on his knee. When the message finished, he turned to the lieutenant beside him. "About ten miles from here, compass bearing two-sixty degrees. That'll be that dry wash we scouted yesterday. They say it looks like a large party."

The lieutenant bawled orders; his men ran from the tents in which they had been sheltering against the sun, and mounted. Within five minutes the detachment was pounding off to the west, leaving their neatly laid-out field headquarters deserted except for four reserve horses and two pack mules.

It did not remain deserted long. As the sound of hoofbeats died away, brush on the perimeter of the camp stirred, and four Apaches stepped out. They quickly loaded guns, ammunition, and supplies onto the mules, heaped what they could not carry into a pile, and set fire to it; one ran among the tents, torching them. Ten minutes later they were heading south at the mules' fastest pace, aiming for the maze of gullies that would hide their trail from any but another Apache.

The dust cloud the heliograph had alerted the cavalrymen to became visible after half an hour's riding; the lieutenant quickened the detachment's pace; the troopers checked their rifles and sabers. From the size of the cloud, it could be a war party big enough to give some sharp fighting.

They came toward the cloud at the full gallop, rifles out, ready for the rehearsed maneuver of wheeling and pouring a devastating first volley into the enemy.

The lieutenant reined up and cursed. Ahead of them an old woman rode a mule which plodded steadily ahead under the burden of several large branches dragging behind it and sending up enough dust for a dozen horses.

The old woman made no complaint when troopers surrounded her, cut the branches loose, and forced her to ride with them back to their headquarters; her face remained impassive at the prospect of captivity. She did, however, allow herself a broad smile at the end of the ride, when she saw the smoldering ruins of the looted camp.

Reflected sunlight bounced from hill to hill, carrying orders and information, sending cavalry units on scouting sweeps, giving routes and objectives. Sweating signalmen squinted and deciphered the flashes. Other eyes watched, noted, interpreted. Morse code manuals were not all that hard to come by.

The warrior ran easily across the sandy stretch. The horse soldiers were not far behind, and would have to come this way, he knew. At the grass-rimmed water hole, without breaking stride, he drew a pouch from his breeches and scattered its contents in the water, then continued running until he was over the brow of a small hill a hundred paces or so away. There he lay and waited, enjoying an excellent view of the water hole.

In half an hour a troop of cavalry approached the hole, stopped, and dismounted. The men ran to the water and dipped their canteens into it; the gurgling sound of the water rushing into the metal containers carried to the warrior, and he smiled.

The men drank greedily. Within minutes, they were down, thrashing in the dust and calling out in shock and agony.

The warrior gave another brief smile, sprang to his feet, and resumed his run.

CHAPTER 12

Horn gave the ditch an admiring look. Copper or such, there didn't seem to be any of that showing, but, taken as a ditch, it was a pretty good, long sonofabitch of a ditch. Or maybe, he thought, tilting the whiskey jug up and letting a good dose trickle down his throat, a sonofaditch. But if you had a sonofaditch, then there ought to be a Mama Ditch and a Papa Ditch, too. What they had here, him and Sieber, wasn't anything more than a poor orphan ditch, just him and old Sieber helping it grow up to be the longest goddam ditch in Arizona Territory.

He raised the jug for another pull, then stopped and cocked his head to one side. "Horses coming."

Sieber listened for a moment, then nodded. "It is so." He reached for the jug. "I told you they beg us back." He hoisted the jug to his mouth and drank. "Well, I ain't going, not for what they paid before." The sound of hoofbeats became louder, and he looked calculatingly at Horn. "How much should I ask for?"

"Double?"

Sieber thought about this for a moment. "Triple." He nodded, satisfied at the prospective demand.

The hoofbeats slowed and halted; there was a jingling and a thump as a rider dismounted. A voice came to them: "Sieber? You down there?" Then Lawton's face appeared, looking down into the ditch.

"Triple wages!" Sieber called triumphantly.

The lieutenant looked baffled. "What?"

"That's what is costs or we don't come back."

Lawton burst into laughter. "Nobody wants you back, you old fool—we're doing just *fine*, thank you!" Horn thought there was something a little forced in his tone.

Sieber reddened and grabbed at the whiskey jug for a quick drink before asking, "Then what the hell you here for?"

"Watch your language," Lawton said. "We escorted a lady out to see you."

Horn and Sieber looked at each other, silently asking what kind of lady would want to visit two disreputable prospectors, and why Lawton would trouble himself to bring her there. There seemed to be no way to answer this while they remained in the mine; Sieber set down the jug and hobbled to where the ditch shallowed and angled up to the surface. Horn followed, grabbing up his worn shirt and shrugging it on.

He was suddenly aware, as he emerged into the sunlight, that he was a sorry sight, dirt-caked and sweaty, a glaring contrast to the dozen smartly uniformed troops of the cavalry escort. Normally he would have enjoyed being a walking offense against military standards of neatness, but the sight of the mounted woman in the elegant riding habit made him regret it. She was a little away from the soldiers, looking down at the puzzled Sieber. Horn, as he approached, thought either I been down in that ditch too long, or that is *some* damn fine woman. It was quite a time since he'd thought about being with a woman, but he found himself thinking quite hard about it right now.

"Are you Mr. Sieber?" the woman asked.

Sieber nodded. "It is so."

"I'm Emmet Crawford's sister."

Sieber looked up at her in surprise. "Ain't you a baby?"

The woman smiled and swung easily off her horse. "Probably I was when you first heard about me. I was just . . ." She stopped and looked at the approaching Horn.

As their eyes met, Horn knew that, lady or whatever, this woman was sizing him up and responding to what she saw. She was pretty, not startlingly so, but enough, with a dignity and frankness in her expression that showed she had class but wasn't worried about making sure everybody knew it. The long glance they were exchanging was a candid avowal that this wasn't the time or place for anything, but, if there ever were a time and place . . .

"This is Emmet Crawford's sister," Sieber said. "Miss Crawford, Mr. Horn."

"How do you do, Mr. Horn?" the woman said. Horn managed a nod. His mouth was suddenly dry and a pulse in his throat was pounding; he suspected that if he tried to speak just then, it would come out a foolish croak. "You knew Emmet too?"

"Some," Horn said huskily.

Miss Crawford turned to Sieber. "I've come to Bowie to settle Emmet's affairs and . . ." She paused, unsure of herself. "Well, you know how soldiers are, they move so much, and I only really knew him through his letters, and he wrote so much about you. . . ."

"Well, I guess we had some times," Sieber said cautiously.

"Yes. And I wanted . . . I just wanted to thank you for being his friend, he didn't have many."

"Both ways it worked," Sieber said.

Miss Crawford looked at Horn, who was aware that he was staring at her very intently, and back to Sieber. When she spoke again, her voice was slightly strained; Horn would have bet that she was feeling that pulse beat in her own throat, too. "I don't want to interrupt you any more than I have; I just wanted to meet you."

"You can stay for lunch," Sieber offered. "We got plenty beans."

"Thank you, that's very sweet, but no . . . I just wanted to say . . . to say that . . ." She stopped and took a deep breath. Horn, watching the sudden swell of the bosom of her dress, felt almost feverishly dizzy. "How did he *die*?" she cried, looking urgently at Sieber. "He couldn't very well write *that* letter!"

Horn cut in quickly. "No pain." She looked at him; her expression held both grief and a reflection of that instant, electric, unvoiced communication between them. "One shot," Horn went on. "He never knew a thing."

She looked at the ground for a moment. "Well. That's good, isn't it?"

When she looked up, Horn held her gaze for another moment, and said flatly, "No."

Horn watched her ride away south with the cavalry escort until they were almost out of sight. Sieber studied him carefully. As they turned to go back down into the ditch, Sieber said, "You probably thought she was pretty because she was your age, but you're wrong. Oh, she was very sad, all right, and that's one thing you want in a woman, but"—he shook his head— "not fat enough."

Horn said nothing, but shucked his shirt, took up his pick, and drove it into the yielding earth with an almost desperate fury.

Shuttling mirrors flung the light of the sun at 186,000 miles a second across plains and hills, dot-dashing news, rumors, sightings, instructions. Toward sunset, a long and urgent heliograph signal sent a party from E Troop pounding out of their field headquarters— this time, with a party left behind to guard the camp. General Miles's officers were capable of learning from experience . . . one experience at a time.

At some distance from the location the message had given, the captain in charge of the party gave the order to dismount. The troopers, rifles held at the ready, moved slowly through the underbrush. In the gloom of early evening, the flickering fires ahead stood out sharply.

"Okay," the captain whispered. "Now, for chrissakes, *no noise.*" He cursed silently as a dislodged pebble rattled; but at least the dodge of wrapping the troopers' spurs with bits of rag was working, and there was no betraying jingle and scrape of metal on rock.

In a few moments they were at the outskirts of the

Indian camp, the standard straggle of untidy branch shelters and small fires. The captain turned to the two lieutenants flanking him and whispered, "That, gentlemen, is why we're going to win. These people are half animal; they can't even set up an orderly camp. Be ready."

In eerie silence—quiet as any damn Apache, the captain thought pridefully—the troopers drifted into the camp, still preserving the advantage of surprise.

The captain saw that all the shelters were covered by his men's weapons, sensed that the decisive moment had come, and seized it. *"None of you move!"* he shouted, his voice reverberating through the camp.

Never was an order better obeyed. No one moved. No one and nothing.

The troopers began to mutter in bewilderment and drift toward the center of the camp.

"What the hell?" said the one lieutenant, glancing around.

"It's a false camp," the other said wonderingly.

"Why the *hell* would they build a thing like that?" the captain said.

The answer was immediate and terrible: a hail of gunfire from the trees surrounding the camp, the dreadful flicker of muzzle blasts like an army of malignant fireflies winking all around them, the irregular thunder of exploding powder; and, within a few seconds, screams of shock and pain.

The captain saw his men, grotesque forms briefly lit by the camp's fires, stumbling, falling, some lifting their rifles to fire aimlessly. The lieutenant by his side said *"Mama!"* and folded in on himself like a jackknife, clutching his belly. The captain pulled out his saber and brandished it, calling, "Rally to me, men!" and ran toward the trees, cursing the day he had received his commission. Leading his troops into a trap like this was something he wouldn't ever live down—once the report went in, his career would be over.

In fact, it ended five yards from the trees, where a heavy slug from an old muzzle-loader took most of the top of his head off.

There were hardly any troopers left standing when, after no more than three minutes, the firing stopped, allowing the moans of the wounded to be heard with frightful clarity.

After a moment there came the distant shrill cry of a bird, answered a little later by another.

"I *swear* this is where the helio signal came from," the lieutenant said fretfully. He reined up and glanced around at his detachment, noting the evident exhaustion of both horses and men—and in this barren spot, they weren't going to find anything to relieve that, for sure.

"I don't get it either," the grizzled sergeant by his side said. He pointed off to the east. "There it is again." The lieutenant looked in the direction of the extended finger and saw a distant, mocking flashing.

Brown hands held the mirror—elegantly framed in rosewood, treasured loot from a long-burned wagon train—and tilted it with delicate precision. The mirror holder's companion squatted beside him and grunted rapid instructions, running one finger over a tattered booklet opened on the ground before him: "Short-short-

short, long-long-long, short-short-long, long, short-short-short-short."

He and the man holding the mirror exchanged tight smiles. It was wonderful what toys the white men brought to war, and the interesting things that could be done with them.

"That's a helluva long ride," the sergeant said as the distant signal concluded.

"We've got to try and make it," the lieutenant answered wearily. He raised his right arm high and brought it down pointing forward; the exhausted troopers shifted in their saddles and urged their reluctant mounts into motion once again.

"Even though," the lieutenant went on slowly, "I think it's all a wild-goose chase."

"How so?" the sergeant asked.

"I'm afraid the Apaches have figured out the helio."

The sergeant looked at him. "Then the whole *thing's* useless, if they have."

"That's right."

"But what'll we do?"

The lieutenant closed his eyes, then opened them and looked ahead at the endless vista of plains and mountains and hard blue sky. "Keep on getting killed, I guess."

CHAPTER 13

"Just you remember, now," Sieber said. "The fat one's mine."

Horn grinned at him. Even in the dusk, as they rode into the outskirts of the mining town of San Simon, he could see his partner's painfully acquired neatness of aspect. Sieber had pounded his clothes clean in a brook, rubbing them on stones Indian-fashion, then spreading them out to dry in the sun, and had hacked his beard into a semblance of evenness. Horn himself had gone to some trouble to spruce up for the jaunt. It had been a long time since he had let off any steam, and he looked to get pretty disheveled in the course of the evening; no harm in starting off with your best foot forward.

Seeing that Miss Crawford, that had brought up a whole lot of stuff that hadn't been bothering him for a while, and tonight, he promised himself, it was going to get worked off.

"Don't worry about me none," he said. "Like that fellow in the poem, Spratt."

"What poem is that?" Sieber asked.

"About this man and his wife, he didn't go for fat meat, she didn't go for lean. So they didn't have no cause to quarrel and between 'em polished off the whole platter."

"Ha!" Sieber said, pleased. "So I'll be *Frau* Spratt, you be the Mister, and we got us a good feast tonight."

They were at the unpainted frame building that conveniently catered to San Simon's needs for wine and women—there was song occasionally, but usually informal and discouraged by the clientele and management—and dismounted. Horn had a fleeting thought of Miss Crawford . . . no fat on *her*, for sure . . . and stepped into the building with a renewed urgency.

By the time the first bottle of whiskey had been drained, things were sorted out nicely. Sieber was squashed into his chair under the bulk of a plump lady in his lap, his voice muffled by the expanse of powdered bosom he was leaning his head against. Horn's lapful was darkly pretty, lighter, and slimmer, but with plenty there to hold on to, and every so often moving gently in his lap enough to signal him pleasantly that *she* knew precisely how glad he was to have here there, and that she appreciated his response.

Horn reached around her for the second bottle and filled the four glasses on the table.

". . . and this man here," Sieber said loudly, his face flushed, resting his arm on the fat woman's shoulder and pointing somewhere near Horn, "with the whole *Messcin Army* shooting at him, he run out and made the rescue, even though he was wounded bad in six placeses."

Horn thought that Sieber looked drunker than he had ever seen him. He considered, too, that he himself *felt* drunker than Sieber had ever seen *him*, so it kind of balanced. He wondered if that would cause any problems later on, upstairs, but his reaction to another shift in position by the girl on his lap reassured him. "Quit makin' it more'n it was," he said. He drained his glass and refilled it. "Inna firsplace, only two of the wounds was serious. And it wasn't the *whole* Mexican Army against me." He looked soberly at the two women. "Just a thousand men." He grinned. Damn, it was *fun* cutting loose with the brags this way. A little whiskey to oil the tongue up, and you could just go on and *on*, impressing the hell out of everybody even if they didn't more than half believe you. He wondered vaguely why, when he was sober, he didn't give a shit about impressing anybody—or, for that matter, having fun."

"I remembered it as more," Sieber said.

"Thass probably because they had all those huge new cannons," Horn said, then shook his head in solemn reproof. "You gotta watch that exaggerating."

The sound of the door from the hall slamming open brought Horn awake, his hand instinctively snaking toward the gun belt draped over the chair on top of his trousers. Then he recognized Sieber's voice, muttering brokenly, "Horrors . . . horrors . . ." The girl next to him mumbled sleepily into the pillow as he moved from under the leg flung across him, struck a match to sputtering light, and lit the wick of the kerosene lamp next to the bed.

Sieber, in long underwear—Horn wondered briefly if the fat lady hadn't found it kind of scratchy—stared wildly at him, eyes wide in the lamplight. "Such nightmares . . ." he said. He spied the opened whiskey bottle next to the lamp, grabbed it, and took a long swallow which ended in a sputter and gasp.

The girl turned and sat up, looking at Sieber with concern. Horn thought that she made a pretty picture, in the soft, warm light, bare to the waist like that—then she cursed and pulled the sheet up to her shoulders as a uniformed man stepped into the room. Evidently what was all right—in the family, so to speak—with paying customers didn't hold for strangers.

The new arrival was Lieutenant Lawton—no, twin bars shone on his shoulders, Horn saw; the bastard had got himself promoted. "All right, you two, come on, get dressed," the freshly minted captain said.

Horn looked at him sourly. "Is a nightmare catching?" he said to Sieber, pried the bottle loose from the older man's grip, and drank.

Lawton ignored this—peering hard, Horn noted, at the sheet covering the girl from the waist up—and said loudly, "General Miles wants you both at Bowie fast—we're having a little trouble with the Indians."

Sieber blinked away the last of the mists of his nightmare and said happily, "I'm an old fool. I work for *quadruple* wages or I don't work. That means four times what it was, in case you don't know the word."

"Will you just *please* get ready?" Lawton said.

Horn slid from under the sheet, disarranging it so that the girl was briefly exposed enough to make the captain's eyes widen before she snatched it up, and began pulling on his clothes. "You got to tell the general," he said cheerfully, "there's a new invention. Called the hee-lee-o-graph. It'll solve all his problems with them Indians, no doubt about it."

Deftly buttoning the front of his trousers, he gave a yelp of laughter; Sieber leaned against the wall and roared with delight. The girl looked from one to the other, and at the tight-faced officer, and giggled. She didn't know what the fun was about, but the laughing got to her, and she could no more help joining in than she could help yawning when somebody else did. And if it made that beady-eyed horse's ass of a soldier mad, so much the better.

The ride from San Simon to Bowie had sobered Horn and Sieber somewhat, but they were still in a mood of mild hilarity as they lounged opposite General Miles at his desk. It was well after midnight, but the general was impeccably dressed in an unrumpled uniform, only the lines on his face showing the strain he felt.

"I may have made an error in dismissing you," he told them. "I admit it. Perhaps there is still a place for civilian scouts. In addition, of course, to my heliograph."

Sieber leered at him. "I bet you haven't caught one warrior."

Mile's face tightened, and he said stiffly, "We have come *close*, on several occasions . . . and arithmetic is not why we're here. I'm sending Captain Lawton"—he nodded toward the rear of the room, where Lawton stood at parade rest—"with my best troops on a major campaign. Geronimo will be run to earth now—I have given my word to the President," he finished impressively.

Horn considered that Geronimo's word, even if somewhat untrustworthy, would be more to the point.

"How long to reassemble your scouts?" Miles asked Sieber.

"Two weeks; maybe less."

"Make it less. I never like to keep the President waiting."

Sieber's mouth twisted as if he were preparing to spit. He looked at Horn. "You stay here for me."

Horn nodded. Some talk with Lawton on the late-night ride had given him the notion that Bowie might be an interesting place to spend some time in. . . .

Sieber rose and made for the door, ignoring Lawton, then stopped and turned to face the general. "General Miles? When you fired me, I said some insulting things about you," he said quietly. "I was angry, my pride was hurt . . ." The general looked at him with slight surprise. "I just want you to know one thing . . . I meant *exactly* what I said."

The flat-roofed civilian store which the Army allowed to operate in Fort Bowie did not boast such refinements as a covered walkway in front of it; but its side cast, about two hours before noon, enough shade to make Horn comfortable as he sat on an upturned barrel, braiding strands of cord together. It would make up into about the best *riata* he had ever put together, he figured—which was as it should be; each time you did a thing you got better at it.

He lifted his head to look at two people approaching the store. Lawton and Miss Crawford, strolling along polite and pretty, officer and lady. He watched the movement of her legs under her skirt, and his fingers faltered in their swift, almost mechanical movement.

Lawton's gaze passed over Horn as if over a rock or a scatter of buffalo chips, something that was part of the landscape but not worth noting. The Crawford girl's eyes locked on Horn's for an instant. It seemed to him that she should say something or acknowledge his presence, or maybe that he should acknowedge hers; he wasn't sure which. The instant passed, and she was inside the store with Lawton.

Horn resumed his braiding, now muttering impatiently over it.

The slice of shadow at the side of the store had diminished perceptibly when Miss Crawford and Lawton emerged, carrying paper-wrapped parcels. They were conversing animatedly; the girl's voice might have been pitched to reach someone just out of sight of the store's front. As she and the captain moved past the corner of the building, her gaze drifted sidewise. The lessening area of shadow was untenanted.

Ernestina Crawford stepped out of the little house on the post that General Miles had thought suitable to her circumstances: not as grand as would have been allotted to the visiting wife of a congressman or field-grade officer, but a cut above what charity would have dictated for an enlisted man's widow; just right, in short, for the bereaved lady relative of a dead minor officer in Bowie for a short stay.

She sniffed hungrily at the still-cool morning air. Back in Boston, there had been sweltering days, but the steamy heat rolling off the Charles had been bearable in a way that the furnace-dry Arizona summer was not. You could dry up inside your clothes out

111

here. She sighed. One way or another, Boston was in her past now, and the future wasn't going to be awfully different from this. . . .

She stopped and stiffened. Ahead of her in the dirt roadway, but carefully not seeing her, Horn stood. A spinning loop of rope made a blur around his legs, then rose up his body, then descended. It seemed to have a life of its own, allowing him to leap out of and back into its flickering circle. The motion of the rope, and the man moving in a complex dance she did not understand, brought a sudden heat and a feeling of slack heaviness to her face.

Horn had registered her emergence from the house out of the corner of his eye, and stepped up the pace of his work with the lariat. He gave himself up to it, working out tricky bits he had never tried before and bringing each of them off perfectly.

When he stopped, sweat starting out on his face and body, and let the rope whisper to the ground, he looked back to where she had been standing. She was walking away from him.

Horn stood for a moment, then slammed the end of the rope his hand held into the dust of the roadway.

It was almost cool again, though the house still held much of the day's heat. Ernestina Crawford wondered vaguely if she ought to change out of the loose cotton wrapper she had put on in the most oppressive part of the afternoon. But it would be time for bed soon, and callers weren't very likely now. In any case, it was voluminous enough to be respectable, even if somewhat informal, in case one of the few officers' wives on the post should choose to drop in for a gossip.

She grimaced at a knock on the door. Company would cut the loneliness, but the women she had met out here seemed to be capable of discussing nothing but the repellant complaints the climate, the food and the water brought about in their ladylike constitutions, or their husbands' prospects of promotion. The only female complaints that interested her were her own, of which, thank God, she had none just now; and the only Army officer she cared about had had his last promotion two months ago, receiving a permanent posting to a shallow grave in Mexico.

She opened the door and drew the wrapper closer around her. Hair slicked down and some of the dust knocked off his clothes, the Horn man was still not easy to confront. "Yes?"

"I was showing off," Horn said.

Ernestina Crawford gave a puzzled shake of her head. "I'm sorry?"

"Today. With the rope."

"Oh." Her eyes flickered past him. There were no early-evening strollers in sight.

"I was trying to make an impression," Horn went on.

Reluctantly, as though it were dangerous but inevitable, she pulled her gaze from the street and looked straight at him. "I see."

"I just wanted you to know that," Horn said.

"Well." Her left hand held the neck of the wrapper bunched. It was silly to feel this way; after all, the wrapper covered her from neck to ankle, a good deal more modest, really, than a lot of dresses. But she felt very strongly the situation of there being nothing under the wrapper but Ernestina; stays and such, they were a kind of armor. "Now I, uh, know that."

"That's right," Horn said, his face stiff—was he, she wondered, holding back a smile? And, if he was, why? "I just told you."

Ernestina Crawford looked at him narrowly. "That's all?"

Damn the man, he *was*, on purpose, not smiling. "I guess," he said.

"You can go, then."

She waited for him to tip his hat, to turn, to walk down the darkening street. She wet her suddenly dry lips with the tip of her tongue and said, "You don't seem to be moving."

"No, ma'am," Horn said gravely. "But you're not closing the door."

Her wide eyes held his as she stepped back. Her left hand clenched tighter on the bunched material of the wrapper; her right jerked in a gesture of invitation for him to enter.

Horn tilted in the straight-backed chair in the kitchen, hooking his feet under the rail that held the porcelain-topped table's legs together. The kitchen was small, so it was natural that Miss Crawford's knee should be almost touching his as she sat across from him.

"You don't want more coffee?" she said.

"Three cups is plenty for me, thank you." There was no clock in the room, so far as he knew, none in the little house; but there was a steady beat in his head, in his body, ticking off the seconds that passed. He felt the way he had sometimes after an all-night drunk that had begun to wear off around three in the morning, drained but alert, seeing things more clearly than at other times. The girl's hand still was clenched on the wrapper at her throat, and he studied the network of blue veins on its back, then the column of her throat, the slightly parted pale lips, the intent gaze, the spill of unbound hair around her face.

"I might just have a touch myself," she said. She tilted the enameled pot, half filling the mug in front of her, then looked back at him, saying nothing.

Horn stirred in his chair under her glance. "What?" he said finally.

"I wasn't sure how to bring it up . . . you see, I didn't know what you did for Emmet when I came to the mine."

"What did I do for Emmet?" Horn asked.

She raised her eyebrows. "You rescued him."

Horn shook his head. "I didn't rescue him. He died."

"Why did you go out after him?"

"Well," Horn said almost defensively, "Sieber couldn't, not with his bad leg."

"Emmet was *nothing* to you," she said, almost urgently, wonderingly.

Horn looked past her at the coal stove, and then at the engraving of Grover Cleveland that hung on one wall of the kitchen. "How long you staying around Bowie?" he said loudly.

She spread the fingers of both hands on the table and clenched them into fists. "Don't change the subject on me—you didn't *have* to do anything, so why did you go after him at all?"

115

Horn looked at her hands for a moment, and finally said, "I couldn't think of any reason not to."

Her right hand slid to the coffee mug in front of her, grasped the handle, and lifted it. The rim touched her parted lips as she looked steadily at Horn. "You sure you don't want any coffee?"

Horn said nothing, and did not nod or shake his head. She took a brief sip from the mug, then set it down. "I don't want it either." Carefully, not spilling any, she tilted the mug and poured its contents back into the pot.

Slick and sweet, she lay along him, not quite beside, not on top, but sort of leaning. Soft places and hard—where her hipbone poked out, and the sweep of her rib cage—fit pleasingly onto him; her hair drifted across his face, and he blew it away with shallow puffs of his breath.

"I haven't done anything like this in a long time," he said, looking into the dark that held them.

"Made love, you mean?" Miss Crawford said. Her mouth moved on his shoulder. He wondered what her name was, but it seemed somehow that they had got past the point where he could ask. Come to that, she didn't know his first name, either. He grinned; that had been quite some goings-on, a few minutes back, for folks that hadn't been properly introduced. "I mean doing it sober," he said.

"If you want to go get drunk, I'll wait for you here," she said drowsily.

He reached an arm around her and pressed her against him. "No, no, this is fine."

Light fingers ran up his chest, digging in very

slightly with buffed, rounded nails. "You sound almost happy, Mr. Horn."

"I won't lie to you, Miss Crawford," Horn said solemnly. "I've been riding and tracking and mining till hell wouldn't have it, and it's hot out and the flies are biting, and even if you were some horrible old sow, I would be happy."

The questing fingers tightened around a curl of hair on his chest, positioned, he could tell, to give one damned painful pull. "I'm not sure, was that a compliment?"

"I was hoping so."

The fingers relaxed, drifted down, down, to lie in a loose grasp. "You can really be very nice."

"Every so often it happens," Horn said. And damn if it wasn't beginning to happen again, if that was what she meant.

"I like you. Will you remember that?"

Horn blinked. "Why remember?"

"I'm leaving Saturday." Tapping fingertips brushed him here and there, especially there.

"Any special reason?" He let his hand slide down her damp back, thumb carefully following each knob on the curved spine.

"I'm getting married next month in Wyoming."

Horn's hand flattened out just at the base of her spine—not withdrawing from her, but suddenly neutral. "Any special reason?"

The dark was not so deep that he could not see the gleam of her teeth as she pushed her hair aside and looked at him with a short smile. "The real truth, as to why I came to Bowie, was to try and decide, was I doing the right thing, getting married." Now he could see only the faint glint of her eyes; the smile was gone. "And, after a lot of thought, I reached the only possible conclusion—I am doing the wrong thing, getting married."

"Sounds to me like you've got a good head on your shoulders, Miss Crawford," Horn said. He inhaled the scent of her hair, a little acrid and sweaty—and no wonder, after all that—but with an underlying sharp sweetness.

She spoke softly, as if talking to herself as much as to him. "I'm marrying a builder, a contractor. He is often dull . . . but always *home*. My brother was a soldier and our father was a soldier and I've have enough of sudden death."

She raised herself on one elbow and looked down at him. "All I want from a man is that he *outlive* me."

She seemed to be waiting for some reply, but Horn could think of none. After a moment she bent to him, seeking his lips with greater hunger than before, then running urgent hands over his body.

CHAPTER 14

"If I was an inventing man," Sieber said, "you know, a long-headed fellow like that Edison or Bell, I think I would figure out a way to do all this riding on some kind of a machine."

"What's wrong with horses?" Horn said, comfortable in the saddle.

Sieber sighed. "An old man like me, bad leg and heavy in the butt, forget that man of iron shit, it gets to you, being on a horse all that time."

Horn grinned at him. Old Sieber could complain as much as he liked; the fact was, he was good for more hard going on the trail than most men half his age.

They were passing the supply wagons now. Sieber looked at the straining mules and said, "Now, that—couldn't some kind of steam engine, only it don't need tracks, do the same job?"

"Maybe," Horn said, "but they'd have to carry so much coal with 'em, there wouldn't be room for anything else."

Sieber grunted and sketched a salute at Micky Free and a contingent of Indian scouts as they cantered by them. They were soon even with and drawing past a troop of cavalry. Horn looked across—and, to his irritation, up—at them. These were Miles's picked men, all massive and muscular, mounted on correspondingly massive and powerful horses. They moved along with an uncanny regularity and discipline. "Don't know but what you got a point," he muttered. "Those guys look about halfway to being machines right now."

It took them a long while to reach the head of the column. If numbers could crush Geronimo, they damned well had the numbers.

Sieber looked somberly at the toiling caravan of men and animals. "Ain't seen anything like this since the War," he said. "Coming in toward Gettysburg, was like a river of us going through one valley, another river in the next, all stretched out as far as you could see. Was a lot of us never come back."

"Well, hell," Horn said. "This ain't the same thing. We ain't up against artillery and Minié balls and bay-onet charges and Robert E. Lee, and all that everyone talks about."

"No," Sieber said grimly. "Just Geronimo. I think maybe we'd be better off going against Lee. I think there is a lot of little-noted nor long-remembered graves ahead of us. Especially with asshole Lawton running this."

They joined Lawton, riding out ahead, without a greeting. Both rode with heads bowed, scanning the ground. Lawton glanced from one to the other, then, after a time, spoke irritably. "When do you figure we'll pick up Geronimo's trail?"

"We already did," Horn said.

Sieber nodded. "Half an hour ago."

"You could have told me," Lawton snapped.

Horn blinked at him and, after a moment said,

"That's right." He directed his gaze once again to the ground.

In midafternoon, Sieber and Horn rode up to a group of the Indian scouts who had been sent out on tracking detail ahead of the column. The scouts were talking animatedly to each other in Apache; some of them pointed to an area of the hard-packed ground.

Horn listened to them for a moment, asked a couple of questions and received the replies, then turned to Sieber. "Way they read the sign, Geronimo's divided his men—some went straight on, some more east. Which way do you want to go?"

"Which way do *you* want to go?" Sieber said. He waited for Horn's reply, then gave a satisfied nod as Horn rode to the spot the scouts had been studying and looked at it intently.

Horn sent his horse ahead, casting to the right and left, all the while examining the apparently featureless ground. After a moment, he turned toward Sieber and called, "I think both ways are wrong—we should go *that* way." He pointed a little west of due south.

Sieber nodded his approval. "Head of the class, Mr. Horn." He stood in his stirrups, turned, and signaled the change of direction to the distant Lawton, then rode after Horn. Behind them, the column slowly snaked its way into the turn.

To the sergeant standing guard, the swirling winds of the night carried only the sound of rustling grass and brush. There was reason to be alert, he knew— this was, after all, hostile territory—but none to be alarmed. The half-moon, obscured by racing clouds,

121

still gave enough light so that he could be sure of detecting any movement in the shadowed shrubbery around the camp.

He turned to look toward the north, wondering if there had been a flicker of motion far off. A shadow rose from the sparse brush behind him; a knife glinted in the fitful moonlight, then darkened as blood from the sergeant's slit throat gushed across it.

The Apache warrior laid his victim quietly on the ground, then turned to survey the cavalry camp. He stepped cautiously among the sleepers, peering at the back of a head here, an upturned face there. He held a rifle at his side, and kept the muzzle sweeping constantly back and forth as he searched.

He stopped, and the rifle steadied. That was the right shape, and the shaggy head was right, too. . . . The sleeper muttered something in the white man's tongue, and shifted; now the moonlight caught the broad, hard face. Sibi. The warrior brought the rifle to his shoulder and brought the front sight to bear between Sieber's closed eyes. His finger squeezed gently on the trigger then convulsed, sending the shot wild, as something cannoned into him. A yell from Sieber told him that the bullet had found a target, if not a mortal one, but he had other matters to occupy him now.

Horn's desperate leap—automatic, triggered by God knew what instinct when the Indian had briefly obscured the moon and awakened him—knocked the Apache off balance. The warrior quickly recovered and brought the clubbed rifle around in a deadly sweep; shouts were already coming from troops awakened by the shot.

Horn threw himself to one side, and the rifle passed just over his head. It was coming around and up for another blow which would smash his skull when Horn thrust his revolver in front of him and fired. The Apache lurched sideways, dropping the rifle, twitched once, and did not move again.

Horn whirled and ran to Sieber, who was sitting up, pawing his blankets away from himself and cursing. "You okay?"

"I am fine," Sieber said. "Only my bad leg is now again my good leg." He pulled the last of the blankets away. In the moonlight, the glistening fast-spreading stain on the thigh of his long underdrawers looked black. He stared at the dead Indian. "They warned they would try to kill me, so I shouldn't be surprised."

Sieber grimaced and breathed heavily as he pressed a cloth pad to the pulsing wound. "You keep saving my life, Mr. Horn. Someday I ought to get around to thanking you for your efforts."

Horn held out a length of cloth to bind the dressing in place. "Why'd they try this? 'Cause they figured no one else could lead us?"

"It is so," Sieber said. "But they failed. By morning, I'll be dancing."

At dawn, the winds were still high, sending dust swirling around the tracking party as they prepared to move out in advance of the troops.

Sieber stood by his horse, the trouser on his wounded leg bulked out by the bandage beneath the cloth. His face was white and drawn. He made as if to mount, but gasped and sagged when he tried to lift the leg.

Horn hurried to him. "Lemme give you a hand."

Sieber glared at him. "I don't need nothing. God-dam horse won't stand still, is all!"

He grabbed at the saddle and tried once more to mount, and once more fell back, unable to stifle a yelp of pain. Horn, to his own astonishment, grabbed the bulky scout and heaved him upward; Sieber grabbed at the saddle horn and pulled himself upright.

He frowned down at Horn. "Mount up, Mr. Horn—*move*. I'm not waiting for you!" Horn shook his head admiringly as Sieber rode off after the scouts, then ran for his horse.

"How is he?" Lawton asked, sending his horse close to Horn's.

Horn looked at him. He supposed it went with the military mind to ask questions you already knew the answer to. "Wounded and old," he said briefly.

"Well," Lawton said brightly, "don't worry about Sieber. Hell, he's been shot twenty-eight times."

Horn nodded once, then stared ahead, to where Sieber rode with the scouts.

Once the trail they were to follow was clear, the scouts and Sieber dropped back to the rear of the column; Horn remained in front with Captain Lawton.

The sun was burning off the morning haze, and heat and dust were rising from the ground. Horn, looking back, could see the tiny figure of Sieber among the scouts; as his own horse's hoofs hit the hard ground and jarred him, he could imagine what each such jolt must be doing to Sieber's wound.

The next time he looked, Sieber was a little away

from the scouts—to one side? No . . . behind. A little later, the distance was greater.

Lawton looked nervously at Horn. "He's falling behind worse all the time."

Horn was too upset to work out a sharp reply to Lawton, said, "Probably what he always does—takes it easy. At the start, I mean."

"You think?" Lawton said eagerly.

Horn nodded. "He didn't get where he got by being dumb." It was some lousy situation, he thought, when he wound up trying to reassure asshole Lawton . . . and not believing a word of what he was saying.

He turned and sent his horse cantering to the rear of the column, past the supply wagon, past the straggle of scouts. Sieber was a good bit behind now, and hoisting Emmet Crawford's battered old flask. Horn rode along beside him silently until Sieber suddenly shuddered and gasped, seeming to be on the point of surrendering to the pain. Horn spoke with calculated scorn. "Looking to get drunk before breakfast?"

Sieber drew a long breath, and said, "It is so." He took another pull at the flask.

"You want my opinion on that?"

"Mr. *Horn*," Sieber said. "I am wounded, I do not want to hear your goddam opinion, I do not want to hear your goddam *voice*. You may think it pleasant getting shot, well, it isn't." Sieber tucked the flask in his jacket pocket.

They rode in silence awhile. Horn saw Sieber shudder and sway; white showed at the bottom of his eyes. Horn spoke loudly: "I think it's just that you're clumsy."

Sieber made a visible effort to concentrate and turned to him. "What?"

"Nobody else gets wounded all the time. This the worst?"

Sieber blinked. "Worst? Worst what?"

"Worst *wound*, for chrissakes."

"Oh, no," Sieber said, more crisply now. "Chato shattered my hip once. It was a great shot—he was on horseback and he fired just the one time . . . wonderful marksmanship." He looked at Horn and took a deep breath. "Thank you, Mr. Horn, I'll be all right now."

"Sure?"

"No." But Sieber gestured for Horn to ride ahead to the front of the column, and was sitting straighter in his saddle.

Horn rode past the scouts, then the equipment wagons. He was even with the soldiers when he heard a cry from behind him: *"Tom!"*

He turned. Sieber, far behind, was sliding slowly from his horse. As Horn watched, he hit the ground and lay limply.

Horn sent his horse pounding back to where Sieber lay, vaulted from it, and knelt beside him.

"I'm done," Sieber said.

"I know."

"Sorry."

Horn slid the flask from Sieber's pocket and put it in the scout's hand. Sieber opened it and drank quickly; the pain lines in his face smoothed a little. "You're on your own now."

"I can do it," Horn said flatly.

"I don't know," Sieber muttered. "I don't know. We talked about him enough. I just wish you was experienced more. Press him, remember that. Got to keep the pressure on."

"I will," Horn said.

"His people, they think he knows the future. They believe that. Press him, work him, no matter what." He laid the flask on the ground beside him and fumbled at his belt. "You got to promise me something." Horn nodded. "You bring him in, you'll be the king of Arizona . . . true. But . . ."

He reached a closed, trembling hand out to Horn. "Take this. Keep it with you."

Horn looked at the razor-sharp hunting knife that quivered in Sieber's grasp. "What for?"

"Because . . . if it goes bad, you got to kill yourself. Don't let them torture you dead."

Horn hesitated. What the Apaches, especially the women, did to prisoners was no picnic. Cut-off eyelids and being staked out for the ants wasn't anywhere near the worst of it. It was funny, getting into this line of work, that he'd never included the possibility of capture and torture in his plans. The job was getting Geronimo, not being gotten by him, and what he'd been paying attention to was how to do that. It made him uneasy to have to work out what to do in case things went disastrously wrong; it took the edge off the concentration you needed to see that they went right.

Sieber's eyes closed, and he spoke weakly but urgently. "I know. Trust me. Promise that you'll kill yourself."

Reluctantly, Horn nodded, and took the knife. It made sense, but the idea still went against the grain.

He tested the blade on the ball of his thumb. It was sharp enough to do the job right, anyhow.

He stood, cupped his hands, and called toward the distant group of scouts, "Micky!"

The little half-breed wheeled his horse and rode hard to where Horn stood over Sieber. Horn pointed back over the route they had traversed. "Take him home."

Micky Free nodded and slipped from his horse, trotting over to kneel by Sieber. As Horn remounted, he noticed that Micky still wore his grin, though less widely. There was some kind of man, Horn thought. Takes everything that happens the same way, as if it was some kind of fun arranged especially for him. He worships Al Sieber, but what he's got his mind on is how to get him back to Bowie alive, and that's an interesting enough proposition to keep him happy. . . . He wondered if Micky Free would kill himself to get out of being tortured. Probably not.

When he rejoined Lawton at the head of the column, the captain looked at him silently. "Sieber's going back to Bowie," Horn said.

"But we need—"

"Sieber's no good for this chase now," Horn said harshly. "Even chance, Micky Free gets him back to the fort in time, they can patch him up. But he wouldn't last another day on this."

He turned and saw Micky Free slowly easing Sieber onto his horse. In the distance, their figures were like one of those Rogers sculpture groups high-toned people had in their parlors—"The Wounded Scout," or some such. If they ever made one of Sieber and Micky, they'd have to work the flask into it some way.

Lawton looked at him anxiously. "Without Sieber, how can we—"

"We can or we can't," Horn said. "You want to turn this circus around and head back for Bowie, you can do that. You can also explain it to General Miles and President Cleveland, and think about selling dress goods for a living. Or you can keep on, like you're supposed to." He smiled wolfishly at the captain. "After all, you got me."

Lawton nodded morosely.

Horn looked back at the train of men and equipment spread out behind him. Lawton didn't count. It was all Horn's now.

CHAPTER 15

The dust cloud ahead drew them like a magnet, pulling them through the murderous heat. The mules were urged to their best speed, but their pace limited that of the whole expedition. The cloud, spotted that morning where Horn's reading of the trail told him it would be, stayed at the same distance throughout the blazing afternoon hours.

"We've got to rest soon," Lawton said.

Horn gestured at the distant dust cloud. "Not till he does." He swung around and glanced down the length of the column. The cavalry, shimmering in the heat haze, were moving more slowly now. He turned back to Lawton. "Come on—we've gotta go faster."

"Don't worry about my men," Lawton said proudly. "These aren't just any troops. General Miles recruited them special. From all over the Southwest. They're the biggest, most powerful men anywhere around." Horn gave him a flat glance. "I can tell you're not impressed."

Horn looked past him at the dust cloud that marked Geronimo's band, and said softly, "The Apaches, when their sons get to be ten, twelve, they give them a swallow of water and then run them. They run their children across the desert. For hours. Kids these are. And the temperature can hit one-twenty, sometimes one-thirty-five. After the run's over, the children have to spit out all the water they've been holding in their mouths. Every drop they were given."

He looked coldly at Lawton. "Impressed? Just 'cause you rounded up some guys with broad shoulders?" He shook his head and rode out away from Lawton.

By dusk the cloud was smaller. Horn cursed as he saw Geronimo's lead increasing, but the column could not be pushed to any greater speed. The only hope of narrowing the gap was to get an early start in the morning, not much past first light.

Horn, mounted, glared ahead in the predawn dimness. Lawton approached him, buttoning his uniform jacket. "What . . . ?"

Horn pointed toward the horizon. Even with the sun not up, it could be seen sharply against the paling sky, a wavering line of low hills. No dust cloud hung in the air to blur any part of it.

"He rode all night," Horn said.

Lawton was taken aback, then brightened. "He'll kill his horses."

Horn looked at him almost with pity. Did the captain honest to God think that Geronimo would have to fill out requisitions for new mounts in triplicate and present them to some goddam Indian supply board? "Don't matter," he said flatly.

Geronimo hadn't quite killed his horses, but they weren't good for much anymore, Horn estimated. The scraggly Indian ponies stood trembling in the broken corral, except for three who were lying down, their sides heaving.

He turned to the dazed rancher, whose eyes kept flicking around the ruins of his property. "Which way did they go?"

"I dunno," the man mumbled. His face was white and slack.

Horn said quietly, almost soothingly, "How many were there?"

"I dunno."

"They took all your horses?"

The rancher nodded slowly.

"How many's that?"

The rancher seemed to try to pull his wits together, but gave up. "I dunno."

The grassland made for easy tracking, and the trail to the next ranch was clear.

The main house was a burned-out shell. In front of it the rancher sat, holding a rifle. A dead white woman lay beside him, several dead Apaches in front of him. He stared straight ahead and did not seem to see the column as it passed.

"They took everything—everything!" the fat rancher said, a week and uncounted miles later, seeming on the point of tears as he looked at the desolation around him.

"How many horses?" Horn asked.

"Hundred, maybe."

"Cattle, too?"

"Goddammit, I say *everything!*"

As they rode off, Horn turned to Lawton and said, "He's getting greedy—it'll slow him down."

Horn looked grimly at the troops behind him. They were keeping going, but only just. A month of the chase had melted some of the beef off them, and the blue of their uniforms was almost completely hidden by ingrained dust.

He looked impatiently ahead and spurred his horse. If the soldiers couldn't keep up with him, the hell with them. It felt good to be moving at top speed for once. He wondered vaguely if Sieber had made it back to Bowie okay . . . if Miss Crawford had gone on to Wyoming to get married up to that contractor. . . . None of that seemed real, now. There wasn't anything but this chase, keeping going, watching for signs on the trail, sweeping the horizon for that damned dust cloud that wasn't ever there. . . . Only, by God, *there it was!*

He stopped and waited for Lawton to catch up with him, then silently pointed. Lawton only nodded, and waved the troops ahead.

The terrain was rougher now. Rocks and scrub brush and the eternal sun slowed them, but the cloud was still there . . . and getting larger.

It was closer than it had ever been, and Horn, well out in the lead, thought he could almost distinguish the shapes of individual horses and men at its base.

The mounted warrior was suddenly, shockingly, there, riding at him from the shelter of a massive rock. Before Horn could react, the Indian whirled a flung tomahawk at him—and was gone, almost before the weapon took him in the shoulder and sent him toppling from his horse.

He lay in the dust and rocks, breathing hoarsely and clutching his shoulder. The tomahawk lay a yard away from him, and he realized that the blunt end of its head had struck him, not the business edge. Which, he considered, was why he was lying there bruised all over and with one *hell* of a sore shoulder, instead of flopping around like an axed chicken while most of his blood drained out.

He was reaching for the tomahawk when Lawton pounded into sight and leaned over to call to him. "You okay?"

Horn gritted his teeth and nodded. He held up the tomahawk and said, forcing a smile, "We're getting him worried."

Lawton seemed almost elated at the sight of the stretch of blazing prairie ahead of them. "What's he trying to do, burn his tracks?" he called to Horn. "I told you we had him worried!"

Without waiting for the fire to die away to smoldering stubble, he set his horse at the flames and pounded ahead, signaling to his dispirited men to follow. Horn got through with only uncomfortably warm boot soles and the stench of burned horsehair to remind him of the ordeal; some of the troopers had raw blisters and charred spots on their fraying uniforms.

A few miles farther on, they came to a small stream which struck Lawton as an ideal camp for the night, even though there were still some hours to darkness; he gave orders for the halt over Horn's protests.

"The men will do better when they're fresh," he

said. "And we can afford losing a little time now. Geronimo will have counted on his little backfire to slow us up, and he'll slacken his pace accordingly. We may be a lot closer to him than he thinks."

"Yeah, well—" Horn said. The rest of his comment was downed by a rattle of gunfire from the rocks and brush around the camp. Lawton staggered and clapped a hand to his side, then recovered and bawled to his men, "Fire at will!"

The startled cavalrymen grabbed their weapons and loosed a ragged volley, which trailed off when there was no answering fire. Horn calculated that the Apaches had fired no more than a dozen shots before breaking off the ambush.

"You hurt?" he asked Lawton.

"Only a graze," the captain said. "They don't shoot very well."

Horn looked past him at the three cavalrymen and the scout who lay unmoving in the middle of the camp. "Well enough."

The dust cloud marking Geronimo's band was not visible the next day, nor, on the rock-strewn hardpan, could Horn make out any trail sign. He dismounted and ran crouched in the blazing sun, eyes questing over the ground.

Lawton rode up to him. "We lost him?"

Horn looked up. "It's possible."

Lawton frowned as Horn bent and began that strange, loping run once more. Hours later, mounted again, and far ahead of the rest, he worked his way across the difficult terrain. He stopped, dropped from his horse, and bent to the ground. His eyes brightened as he studied the scattered rocks.

He sprang back on his horse and sent it up a slope nearby. From the slight eminence, he could see a few miles farther . . . and there, catching the sun, and not all that far off, either, was the cloud. He grinned. Lawton and his bullyboys might not be the best at this, but they were hanging on. Geronimo was being worn down. . . . "Keep pressuring him," Sieber used to say. Well, they were by God pressuring the old fox, half a summer and nobody knew how many hundreds of miles of pressure, and it was starting to show. They would have him yet . . . *he* would have him yet.

"We've got him," Lawton whispered. In the gloom of early evening, the flickering fires ahead stood out sharply. "That could be his whole force, right there."

Horn looked at him, and at the Indian camp with the scatter of fires and shelters of interlaced branches. As Lawton turned and made urgent gestures to his dismounted troopers to approach silently, Horn slipped away and conferred urgently with two of the Apache scouts.

He pulled a revolver from its holster, grabbed another that was thrust into the waistband of his trousers, and ran forward, brandishing and firing them and yelling.

Lawton whirled angrily as Horn approached him. "We had him! You've messed it up—we've lost surprise. . . ." He stopped, taking in two pieces of information at once. Nothing stirred in the camp that Horn's fusillade should have brought to dangerous life; and a patter of retreating hoofbeats could be heard from the far side of the clearing in which the camp . . . the trap . . . had been set. That was how they had done McLanahan, a fake camp—opening up a captaincy for Henry Lawton, as it happened—and now they had damned near done it to Henry Lawton. He took a deep breath and said, "Sorry."

Horn considered that maybe Sieber hadn't looked at every angle of it. In the words of the master, all soldiers was assholes. But there were assholes and there were assholes. Give him his due, Lawton could, if you set it up for him, work out something pretty sensible. The whole cavalry detachment, what there was of them by this time, was neatly spread out in a horseshoe formation commanding what had to be the genuine article, the camp of Geronimo and his remaining braves. A fast volley into the Apaches—everybody under strict orders to shoot wide of Geronimo, otherwise there'd be nobody to surrender who counted worth a damn—and the whole thing would be at last done and done. Lawton and his beef critters had come through after all. And, just to show that the luck had changed, after a month or two or however the hell long it had been, it was for once cool . . . and dim. . . . Horn flipped from the prone position, in which he had been covering the Indian camp, onto his back. Towering thunderheads stood above him and leaned toward him, sliding across the sky as if they were being pulled on strings, blotting out the sun, churning and tumbling at their edges, bloating to swallow the sky. "Lawton!" he called urgently. "Now!"

"We have to—" Lawton said. Horn never knew if he finished the sentence. Fat drops of rain impacted around him with the force of bullets, then the skies opened with a steady, drenching drumming that flattened him to the earth, dry one instant, an ooze of mud the next. A silvery gray curtain hid the camp—hid everything more than a body length away—from him. He twisted until his rifle lay beneath him, cursing monotonously and without invention. The goddam chase after goddam Geronimo had gone on into the goddam rainy season, and there was goddam nothing they could do about it.

A few hours ago, Horn would have been ready to cut someone's throat for all this moisture—he could feel his body plumping out like a dried raisin dipped in a glass of water as the rain pelted him—but he could have stayed parched five minutes longer and got the whole goddam business *over* with, just as easy. Goddam Geronimo must have an in with the goddam rain god.

After a little over an hour, the sky turned from gray to light gray, and the clouds drifted off to the east. The rain slackened, then stopped, and the Indian camp could be seen once again.

Empty, what else?

A mocking sunset streaked the deserted camp with orange. Horn clawed his way to his feet and slammed his rifle into the ground—then cursed yet again and snatched it up. Now it was coated with mud, and would have to be cleaned before it would be any good.

Horn breathed gaspingly in the steady rain. The rain seemed to hit the ground with a steady ringing sound, or maybe the sound was inside his head, he

couldn't be sure. There was a stream ahead of him, or
what used to be a stream. Now it was a muddy tor-
rent, lapping far past what had been its bank, glee-
fully swollen by the unending rains. He saw troopers
pushing their horses across the turbid flood, some getting across, some not, pulled downstream with faint,
thin cries before they slid beneath the roiling brown
surface. The horses screamed more loudly than the
men, which struck Horn as odd, since it seemed to
him the men had more to lose. But maybe the horses
had their own viewpoint about that.

It was hot, even with the rain, but Horn shivered.
Maybe he had a fever, maybe not. It didn't seem to
matter. Out ahead of the column—there was a lot less
of it now, easier to keep it all in sight—he gestured for
a sharp right turn.

Lawton rode up to him. There was very little left of
his former jauntiness, but, Horn thought, there was
something pretty much like a man showing through
now, with all the spit and polish worn off. "You lost
him again?" Lawton asked. Horn shook his head.
"Then what is this?"

"We're not gonna follow dead on anymore—just
cross his path twice a day, morning and night."

Lawton stared at him. "You mean work twice as
hard, ride twice as far?"

Horn nodded and shivered again. "That's right."
Another chill racked his body. "But he'll think he's lost
us, except at the end of each day, there we'll be." He
gave a cracked laugh. "We'll drive him crazy!"

Lawton looked narrowly at Horn. Horn might be

139

planning to drive Geronimo crazy, but it looked a little as though he was doing a little advance scouting into the territory of madness himself.

Horn shivered again and rode ahead into the rain.

CHAPTER 16

Horn stopped and looked down at the dead Indian. A young man, in spite of the emaciation that aged his face, with something familiar about him. After a moment Horn recognized him as the one who had warned Sieber, that time when Horn was cooking breakfast. A long time ago, a long way away. Sieber was out of it now, and so were a lot of Indians and whites. But there were enough left for it to go on.

He wondered dimly if he could have kept going without the fever burning in him, curtaining him off a little from the rain and fatigue, dulling his awareness of everything but what he needed to know and observe for the job.

He passed half a dozen cattle standing in the downpour, gaunt and sickly. Geronimo was wearing down, too, running short, just as they were.

He wheeled as a sound like corn being popped on a stove came from behind him. Through the sheets of rain he saw horses rearing, soldiers firing and falling. Then the fight was over, and six or so Apaches lay dead beside the trail. Horn rode on through the rain.

* * *

His clothes were still damp, but the sun was drying them, steaming him inside them. He could hear, for the first time since the rain had hit them, talking, even a laugh once, drifting to him from the troopers. The fever was gone now, and he was fully aware of just how bone-tired he was.

He stopped at the crest of a hill and looked ahead. He was going to get a lot tireder, he could see that.

Lawton joined him. "He's picked the worst terrain on purpose, hasn't he?" the captain said.

Horn nodded. "He wants to kill us in the desert." He rode down the hill and into the waste of sand ahead.

Dead Indians marked Geronimo's path through the desert, mostly old men sprawling in the sand where they had fallen. The cavalry left its own trail of hastily dug graves and unburied horses—sunstroke, exhaustion, fever, one scorpion sting thinned its ranks steadily.

But they moved ahead, slowly, painfully, day by horrible day, night by night. Geronimo's dust cloud stayed ahead of them, smaller than it had been, even though it was closer.

At dawn, Horn knelt and studied the droppings Geronimo's horses had left, calculating how far ahead the Apaches must be.

Lawton staggered up to him and looked down, then stared around wildly at the endless desert ahead and the remnants of his command. His voice was high-pitched with strain as he said bitterly, *"What kind of a world is it when our lives depend on horseshit?"*

* * *

"Anyone with infected clothes, come on," Horn said softly. He stirred a large anthill with a stick.

A soldier, stripped to his underwear, handed Horn his tattered uniform. Horn dropped it on the anthill. "Ants love cooties."

They were all walking now. The few horses strong enough to carry a rider were laden with the small store of remaining supplies or the limp forms of the sickest men.

The sand burned through the soles of Horn's boots and reflected heat and glare up into his face, which felt swollen. His eyes stung constantly. He turned to Lawton, grimly plodding beside him, and said, "Henry?" Lawton looked at him. "When are we?"

He knew that the question didn't make much sense, but couldn't think, right then, of another way to put it. Lawton must have been as groggy as Horn, since he seemed to have no trouble understanding it. "June or July," he said, then thought for a moment. "August, maybe."

Horn nodded. "That's what I thought."

Horn smiled thinly. The desert was littered with weapons, clothes, even food. Geronimo was dumping everything now, just to keep going, keep ahead. His smile broadened as he looked along the line of abandoned supplies. It pointed straight to a low line of mountains . . . that marked, at last, the end of the desert.

Horn pointed toward the mountains. "Henry? You know what I think?" Lawton shook his head numbly.

"He's hiding in those mountains. And you know what else?"

Lawton managed an inquiring croak.

Horn looked almost awed as he said slowly, *"We didn't die."*

The troopers, the Indian scouts, and Lawton were in a sleep as deep as if induced by drugs. Horn stirred restlessly in the predawn dimness, and looked around the camp at the base of the mountains. Lawton wanted to rest up for a day, then push on. That made sense, the men needed it, but . . .

He rose from where he was lying, picked up his rifle, and walked toward where his horse stood tethered to a tree. He led it away from the camp, and did not mount until he was out of earshot, then rode into the foothills.

He found a steep path and followed it up. He glanced around constantly, alert for sound or movement.

A little way up the path, he rode under a tree branch stretching over him like an uplifted arm. A bird cry came, then another. He nodded, scanning the trees on both sides of the path. He did not need to be able to see through them to know that one or more warriors were there, watching him.

Farther along, there was a shadow on a rock; it melted away as he approached it. In a small clearing there, he dismounted and tied his horse to a stunted tree. He unslung his rifle and slowly, each movement distinct, laid it against the tree. He hesitated for a moment, then unbuckled his gun belt and laid it, with the holstered revolver, over the horse's saddle.

The path he had been following led ahead and down. He walked along it, not hurrying, not faltering. Another bird cry sounded, closer to him than the others had been. He brushed his fingertips over the front of his shirt where it was tucked into his waistband, and felt the slim, solid shape of Sieber's knife. It was where he could get to it quickly if he had to.

At the next turn in the path he faced two Apaches, both holding rifles. They looked at him silently. One pointed to a smaller path forking off to the right. Horn walked past them and took the path.

It led to a slight crest. When he topped it, he was looking down into a natural bowl in the rock of the mountain. Beyond, he could see a glint that had to be the Baviste River. The bowl was ringed with a dozen armed warriors, standing statue-still. It seemed to Horn that he had come a very long way, and he was surprised to see that the sun was barely up.

An ancient woman sat like a bundle of rags halfway up the side of the bowl. Horn paid no attention to her, but looked toward its center, where a man—old, but even at this distance exuding an aura of power—sat on his haunches.

Horn slowly made his way down the side of the rock bowl, then, at the small level area at the bottom, walked toward the old man, who only now lifted his head to look at Horn.

He had no doubt that, at last, he was face to face with Geronimo.

It was what he had been after, what he had been killing himself for, what he had killed men for, these last terrible months, but there was no denying that it was an uncomfortable situation. He nodded a greeting.

Geronimo did not return it. His eyes revealed nothing as he stared at Horn. They might have belonged to a statue.

Horn sank to his haunches and waited. There was nothing else to do.

Geronimo's lips moved as he uttered a single harsh cry. In response, the warriors began to chant. The rocky bowl seemed to focus the sound on Horn, sending it at him in waves he could almost feel.

The chant rose higher and louder, building, Horn knew, to a climax. What it would be, he had no way of knowing. He fingered Sieber's knife inside his shirt.

Geronimo made an abrupt gesture with his right hand. A warrior on the rim of the bowl brought up his rifle and fired. The bullet whipped by Horn's head close enough for him to feel the wind of its passage and struck dust from a rock a few yards away; he did not move.

Geronimo gestured again; another warrior fired, again nearly grazing Horn. After the third and fourth shots, the firing was constant. Geronimo, still expressionless, stared at him.

Horn, blinking involuntarily at the rattle of the fusillade and the ugly whipping noise of the near misses, suddenly smiled broadly at Geronimo. Pitching his voice to reach the warriors, but not taking his eyes from their chief, he called in Apache, "When you're done playing games, we can start."

Geronimo studied Horn for a second, then lifted his head and cried out to his men. The guns were instantly stilled.

In the sudden silence, Geronimo stared at Horn, unblinking. Horn stared back, keeping his mind blank, waiting.

Without warning, Geronimo began to speak.

The armed braves at the rim of the bowl stood stoically as the sun rose higher, then beat down on their heads from straight above, then began its slide down to the west.

As the heat of the day built and waned, Horn listened to the old man's harangue, the story of his people and their glories, the injustice they had suffered, their beliefs and customs. It was, in a way, he knew, an initiation into the tribe, an ordeal and instruction combined, a rite he must undergo before he could be talked to as a person and not an alien white. Twice, in the heat of the day, fatigue almost took him and his eyes closed briefly, but Geronimo's sudden shout brought him back to awareness.

It was after darkness had fallen and, at Geronimo's orders, a small fire lit next to where they squatted, that Horn sensed that he had passed the test, that the real business could begin.

"I was with a mother I cared for," Geronimo said, "a wife I loved much, and a baby, and another, and another. It was a life of quiet. My mother called me 'the one who yawned.'" His voice rose in intensity. "And then the whiteskins—the whiteskins in one day—they killed my mother—they killed my mother and my wife—my mother and my wife *and my baby and my baby. and. my. baby.*" He stopped and breathed deeply. "The Mexicans say we are terrible enemies. That was what I dreamed of from that day on. And I

147

have become war chief because I was more deeply
wronged than the others." He stared at Horn. "And
now you come to me and say, 'Surrender.'"

"Yes."

"And give up my freedom."

"You call these last months freedom?" Horn asked.

"Why should I surrender?"

"Because," Horn said, "we have five thousand warriors and you have nineteen."

Geronimo said nothing for a moment, then, "A Chiricahua can run seventy miles a day. Can a whiteskin?"

"No. But we have five thousand warriors and you
have nineteen."

"When we attack, it is a massacre; when you attack,
it is a battle. Is that just?"

"No. But we have five thousand warriors and you
have nineteen."

Geronimo said slowly, "You pay twenty dollars for
the scalp of an Indian baby. And you call us cruel. And
to such a people you say I should surrender."

"No," Horn said. Geronimo looked quickly at him.
"I say," he went on, raising his voice, "you *must* surrender."

He leaned forward on his haunches, speaking more
quickly and forcefully. "I'm not saying it's right—but
they don't care if it's wrong, because there are five
thousand of them. And if that isn't enough, General
Miles will just bring in five thousand more cavalry."

Geronimo opened his mouth to speak, but stopped
and continued listening. "So you can die here in the
mountains, or you can surrender and live in peace
back on your reservation—*I give you my word on
that*—surrender and you can stay in Arizona."

In the firelight, Geronimo's face looked as if something beneath the skin were pulling it out of shape.

"That's all there is," Horn said. "Die running or live in peace on the reservation. I know it's not much of a choice, but it's the only one you've got." He was breathing rapidly now, knowing that the moment was here, and almost shouted his next words: "*Now you choose.*"

Geronimo rose and stood by a boulder. Horn glanced up at the rim of the bowl, where the armed warriors were silhouetted against the night sky. He slid his right hand again to touch Sieber's knife.

Geronimo's hands shot into the air above his head, then clenched and began a slow descent. He brought them down, clenching them tighter; his eyes were squeezed shut and his teeth clamped together.

His fists slammed into the boulder with such force that Horn almost expected the rock to split.

Horn relaxed and closed his eyes for a second. He eased himself to his feet, stiff after so long in the same position, and faced Geronimo, seeing him suddenly as a dazed old man. "You have chosen what you had to choose. Now that is done, you must see to your people."

Geronimo nodded and turned, starting to climb up the side of the rock bowl.

CHAPTER 17

"Bowie," Horn said.

Geronimo, riding beside him, nodded. The post, with its neat wooden buildings and its fluttering American and regimental flags, stood out clearly on the flat land. He looked ahead at the line of mounted men drawn up some distance in front of the fort. "There are as many to meet us as there are of us," he said in Apache.

Horn looked back at the straggling line of troopers, scouts, and captives, one group hardly distinguishable from another, the whites burned as dark as the Indians and nobody dressed in anything better than tatters. There were a few more of them than in the reception party ahead, but not many. . . .

"Lawton rode fast, to get there ahead of us and arrange this honor." Geronimo's voice was heavy with irony. On the long ride into captivity, the Apache chief had formed his opinion of the captain, and it was not a flattering one.

"Lawton rides fast whenever there is good news to bring to a general," Horn said. "That is how, in our army, a leader of a hundred gets to be a leader of a thousand."

Geronimo looked at the emaciated hounds that, miraculously, had survived the long chase and the ride to Bowie, and still kept pace with his horse. "It is also how a dog gets an extra piece of meat from its master."

Horn looked ahead and grinned. He could make out Lawton, now, next to Miles in the middle of the lines of mounted officers. Tall in the saddle . . . and, for sure, wagging his tail. . . .

But, he thought, that had nothing to do with it. What counted was that Tom Horn had taken on an impossible job, and done it. Whatever bones and scraps Nelson A. Miles was tossing around didn't count alongside that.

Sieber, on crutches, stood at the rear of the throng of officers and enlisted men in front of the main building on the post. He glanced irritably at Horn, who sat on a bench in the shade, a corner of the building cutting him off from a view of the proceedings. Again braiding on that damned rope, he thought. A normal man, he'd be out here, waiting to see this, waiting for the glory. I bet, when they call for him, he don't even bother to step up. . . .

Lawton, his deep tan contrasting effectively with his resplendent new uniform, stood on the building's porch, addressing the crowd. On a table next to him was a long package wrapped in brown paper.

"Listen, everybody," he said, almost shyly. "I don't like surprises and I don't suppose you do, so let me just get to it. Something very unusual happened here at Bowie, and I don't think it ought to go unnoticed."

Sieber looked again at Horn. *He* seems to be unnoticing it pretty good, Sieber told himself.

"Now the telegraph has started flashing the news across the country, and this is going to be a very famous man I'm talking about—but before his hat size starts enlarging, let me just say one thing."

Lawton glanced out over the heads of the crowd at Sieber, then toward the corner that hid Horn from his sight. "I haven't always agreed with this man, but I'll tell you this—the more we've been together, the more some of the crazy things he did turned out to be right." The crowd was completely quiet now. Sieber looked toward Horn, who still seemed totally indifferent.

"Gentlemen, this isn't a man who pays much attention to ceremony—so what else is for me to say but this . . ." He paused impressively. *"Here's the man who captured Geronimo . . . General Nelson Miles."*

Smiling broadly, Miles stepped out of the building's front door and stood on the porch. Sieber's jaw dropped and he swayed on his crutches as the crowd, led by Lawton, began clapping.

Lawton then turned to the paper-wrapped object beside him, and undid it, revealing a large silver sword, which he gravely handed to the general. Miles raised it high in a triumphant salute.

Sieber looked wildly at Horn. That Horn was rocking on the bench, convulsed with laughter, only deepened his rage. He turned to the porch and bawled out, "Give us the *details*, General! How was it in the desert? Tell us how your ass froze in the rain!"

As Sieber began to speak, Horn left the bench and moved toward him. "Easy," he said.

Sieber turned to him. "But it was you—"

"*Just take it easy.*"

"You are getting *screwed.*"

Horn grinned. "It happens to everyone, you live long enough."

Miles laid the sword down and raised his hands for quiet; the applause died away. "It was my job, it needed doing, I did it," he said; he was obliged to raise his hands to still the renewed outbreak of clapping in appreciation of his soldierly simplicity. "Please." When it was fully quiet again, he went on, "I would rather be remembered as the man who brought lasting peace to Arizona than for the Geronimo capture. So, with the thoughts of peace foremost in my mind, I have ordered all Apaches, hostiles and otherwise, to be immediately taken by train to Central Florida for the rest of their natural lives—"

Horn felt almost as though he had taken a bullet in the gut. Sieber yelled to the general, "That's *swampland,* Central Florida—these are desert people! You send them there, you'll kill them all!"

Horn called out, "*I gave my word they'd stay here!*"

The smile on General Nelson A. Miles's face broadened. It was reflected on that of Captain Henry W. Lawton.

Glaring white light flashed in Geronimo's face, and a cloud of smoke drifted away. He stood impassively as the grinning soldier next to him stepped away and another took his place and posed for the photographer. The new arrival reached out and straightened

153

the draggled travesty of a Sioux war bonnet that the photographer had placed on Geronimo's head.

Behind him, soldiers herded his people onto the waiting train. Women, old men, the few remaining braves, children . . . even the scouts who had tracked him. General Miles's orders had been clear on that point—"hostiles and otherwise."

Micky Free, glaring incredulously from his one eye, was learning what it was to be an "otherwise" as the soldiers he had worked with grabbed him and shoved him up the stairs of the wooden passenger car. He saw Sieber and Horn fighting their way through the mob and called out to them, screaming more loudly as he saw that they did not see him; then a large hand planted itself in the middle of his chest and pushed him into the crowded car.

Horn elbowed, shoved, and kicked a path toward where Geronimo stood; Sieber hobbled behind him, from time to time jabbing with his crutch to clear his way.

Horn burst through to Geronimo, snatched the feathered headdress from him, and threw it away. As he grasped the chief's shoulders, a cavalryman—one of those he had led on the chase, he noted bitterly—ripped his hand from its grip.

"Goddammit," he shouted to the soldier, "I gave my word—he's not going anywhere!"

He caught hold of Geronimo again, and another cavalryman—also a survivor of the chase—pulled his hand away. Horn exploded a punch into the soldier's face and the man went down.

Shouts and yells came from the crowd of civilians and soldiers; the photographer grabbed his camera

154

and scuttled to one side, the legs of the tripod swinging wildly and downing an oncoming trooper. Others leaped for Horn as he slammed a hard right into the first cavalryman's face, exulting in the crunch of bone under his fist. He whirled, snapped the toe of a boot into one's knee, drove an elbow into another's nose.

They fell away and were replaced by two armed troopers. One of them swung his rifle butt at Horn; Horn grabbed it, carried the swing back to bounce off the trooper's head, then turned it on his companion with a savage blow that sent the soldier reeling.

The trooper who had been waiting to be photographed with Geronimo grabbed the Apache chief, and, with the aid of half a dozen others, began hustling him toward the train.

Horn broke away from the surrounding cavalrymen and made for Geronimo; one grabbed him from behind and was tossed to the ground as Horn caught his arm, ducked, and whirled.

The heat, the blows, the startled yells of the crowd, the desperation he felt . . . they all seemed somehow to connect with the long months of the chase. But now, without the fever, the fatigue, the ultimate call on his endurance, it seemed to him that it was worse. What he fought was not the angry cavalrymen—men whose lives he had saved a dozen times over, not that *that* counted for anything now—but what lay behind them. Like Geronimo, he was up against the power that could field five thousand troops or ten thousand, no matter how many he battered out of his way.

But *somehow*, he was almost to Geronimo, the soldiers falling away from him like ninepins as he flailed.

The locomotive at the head of the train gave an explosive snort; the giant driving wheels slid on the track, then caught, and the train jerked ahead. Geronimo was startled—frightened, it broke Horn's heart to see—by the sudden sound, and looked toward him, bewildered, reaching out a hand, as if the man who had broken him could help him now.

He heaved away the soldiers who were trying to hold him and burst out toward Geronimo. His head seemed to explode as something hit it, and he staggered forward.

Lawton grimaced as he slammed his rifle butt against Horn's head once more.

Geronimo's feet were not touching the ground. The soldiers' hands were all over him, thrusting him up into the car. The last thing he saw was Horn falling to the ground, pounded by a dozen rifle butts. They were the men Horn had led through the tortures he, Geronimo, had devised, yet they were hurting him. Geronimo could not understand this, any more than he could understand why a chief of ten thousand, like Miles, would break a sworn word.

Sieber struck out with his crutches, bulling his way through to where Horn lay under the pistonlike fall of the rifle butts; he fell on Horn's body, shielding it, and taking the blows meant for it.

The locomotive's driving wheels turned faster and faster, and the train moved ahead. Now, where white men and red had mingled in confusion a few moments before, only whites stood . . . or, as with Horn and the suddenly battered Sieber, lay. Sieber heard a yelping noise cutting through the chug of the train, and peered blearily after it.

A group of lean hounds, Geronimo's hounds, were

following it, picking up speed to keep pace as it gained momentum.

It seemed to Sieber in that blurred, painful, betrayed moment that the dogs might by some supernatural dispensation follow the train all the way to Florida. He hoped so.

The young private led Sieber to the cell in the Fort Bowie stockade. Sieber, adept at the use of his crutches after three months on them, was pleased at how well he managed to hold the two sacks, one in each hand, as he stumped along.

Near the cell, Sieber stopped and gave an emphatic jerk of his head to his escort. "Yessir, Mr. Sieber," the private whispered, and walked back the way he had come.

Sieber moved ahead until he could see through the barred door of the cell. Horn, in shirt sleeves, was looking out of the tiny window. With his back still turned to Sieber, he called, "What's in the bags?"

Once, when Sieber had first recruited the Talking Boy, he might have been taken aback by something like that. But he had known Horn long enough and well enough now not to be surprised by anything the man came up with. He merely answered, matter-of-factly, "Goods. Blessings."

He set both bags on the flagged floor of the corridor and fished from one a bottle of whiskey, which he thrust through the bars of the door. "Holy water," he said.

Horn took it, pulled the cork and threw it aside, and, with several quick, urgent swallows, began to demonstrate why he would not be likely to have any further use for it.

"Everything is all right, Mr. Horn?" Sieber asked.

Horn took the bottle from his lips, exhaled gustily, and said, "You can't hurt a Christian."

"I checked around," Sieber said. "They let you go, a few days more."

"*White* of 'em," Horn said, raising the bottle again.

"Then I show you what we do," Sieber said excitedly.

He leaned down on the crutches, stretching one hand into the mouth of the other bag, and brought out a handful of coarse dirt mixed with fragments of metal. "Our copper mine—you see? Soon, very close now, a strike."

"*Your* copper mine," Horn said.

"I give you half."

Horn turned and crossed the narrow space of the cell. Holding the whiskey bottle close to him, he stared out between the bars of the small window.

Sieber looked at him with growing concern. "Half is fair. . . ."

Horn whirled and released the anger that had been building in him for a day, ever since Geronimo and the others had been dragged onto the train that was even now carrying them away from their homeland to a fetid swamp. "Nothing is fair!" he shouted.

"Yes . . . wait . . ." Sieber said.

"Even if you *got* a strike," Horn yelled, "you'd get used. Someone would smart you out of it!"

He clenched his teeth and seemed about to smash the whiskey bottle against the bars of the cell door, but drank from it instead. *'I'm done being used!*" he said thickly; Sieber could not tell if the thickness came from rage or the drink. "Done"—he took another swallow—"being"—and another—"*used.*"

Sieber watched him, worried. "What for you next, then?"

Horn said nothing, but tilted the bottle high, his Adam's apple working rhythmically until the liquor was gone.

"I worry for you, Mr. Horn," Sieber said quietly.

Horn opened his mouth wide; his eyes were staring blankly. What he said came out as a hoarse cry: "Worry . . . for . . . the . . . other . . . guy!"

He glared at Sieber, past Sieber at someone or something Sieber thought he must be seeing in the shadows of the corridor, raised the empty whiskey bottle high, and smashed it down on the back of the single chair in the cell, sending fragments of glass spraying through the cell and into the corridor. His fist unclenched, and the jagged neck of the bottle fell to the cell floor.

Horn stood for a moment, his eyes bright in the shadowed cell, then picked up the heavy chair and smashed it against the bars of the window. Sieber winced at the tortured, rending sound it made. Horn swung the chair again; it almost bounced from his grasp, but now it had begun to deform and splinter.

He's breaking Miles's head? Sieber wondered. Lawton's? Mine? His? Again and again Horn brought the chair against the bars until only two splintered legs remained in his hands.

He turned to Sieber, panting heavily, staring at him. Sieber knew that the desperate gulping for breath did not come from exertion.

CHAPTER 18

A long time ago, Cheyenne had been a wild and woolly town, with shootings a commonplace of life. Now, the capital of a state fully ten years old, it was more sedate, with government offices, traction lines, a Carnegie Free Library, and other appurtenances of civilization. One of the few recent episodes of gunplay had arisen out of a saloon dispute, six months ago, over whether the new year of 1900 marked the first year of the twentieth century or the last of the nineteenth.

Whichever had been right, the twentieth century was clearly arriving in Cheyenne. In front of a smithy on a side street stood a large freight wagon; crated on it was a glittering contraption of brass and brightly painted sheet metal supported on four yellow-spoked wheels.

The blacksmith and three helpers set stout planks slanting from the wagon bed to the muddy street. One sprang onto the wagon and knocked out the back of the crate. Carefully the smith and his companions rolled the auto out and eased it down.

Horn, riding by, smiled briefly. Sharp fellow, that

smith, he thought. If cars were going to start competing with horses, he meant to have a corner on both.

He looked ahead. That was the name he'd been given, the Irwin Hotel. He dismounted, hitched his horse to the rack outside the unpretentious building, and entered it.

The woman behind the desk watched him as he signed the register. He noted her appearance briefly, as he did with all women he encountered. This one was nothing special, pushing forty, plain dress, hair pinned tight against her head, kind of a used-up look.

He finished signing, and she handed him his room key. As he turned to leave, she spoke to him loudly: "Mr. Horn?"

He turned quickly. The woman seemed, for some reason, flustered. "I only just wondered," she said, "would you be . . ." She took a quick breath. "How long will you be staying?"

"Depends."

The woman's hands moved nervously on the desk. "I'm . . . Ernestina Irwin's my name . . . the widow Irwin." She gave a quick laugh. "See how cleverly I worked that in?"

"I have an appointment, Mrs. Irwin," Horn said, wondering if the woman was completely balanced. "If it's all right with you, I'd like to clean up."

"Of course, of course—please," she said quickly.

"Thank you." Horn turned away again, then back as the woman spoke once more.

"I hope your room is all right."

"I don't require much," Horn said, trying for patience.

"Well, if it isn't, I can always shift you around. . . ."

"Very kind." He started to turn.

"Tom, dear God, *why don't you remember me?*"

Horn whirled and stared. The woman's face was still as unremarkable and unfamiliar as it had been. There had been a lot of women for him, in a lot of places, and no particular reason for him to remember most of them for long.

Mrs. Irwin took a deep, shuddering breath and, her voice under control once more, said, "My name used to be Crawford and . . . in Arizona once, we . . ." She searched for the word. "We were involved."

Horn looked intently at her. Emmet Crawford's sister . . . a cup of coffee poured back into the pot, a cotton wrapper rustling to the floor, and then . . . some pretty thoroughgoing involving, all right. Fourteen years back, just before the big chase after Geronimo, that was. Those years hadn't done her much good, from what he could see, but then, they never seemed to do anybody much good. Not Tom Horn, for sure. "I'm sorry," he said quietly.

"I haven't changed that much," she said. "You haven't."

He let both transparent lies pass. "Mind," he said vaguely and shrugged. "Just not thinking."

"I been following . . . I've heard a lot about you."

"Whatever you heard," Horn said, "don't believe it."

"Just the good parts."

"Were there any?" Horn said incuriously.

"From time to time." She saw that he was again studying her face. "What?"

"Hair . . ."

"What about my hair?" She reached up and smoothed it.

"Wasn't it long then?"

"It still is, I just wear it up."

"Oh." He continued looking at her, considering. "Prettier down."

She looked away in confusion. She had not been able to keep from demanding that he notice her; but now that he had, his attention was making her uneasy. "Well, it really is unpredictable, isn't it?" she said.

"What?"

"Life."

Horn looked at her expressionlessly. "How was yours?"

She closed her eyes briefly, then opened them. Horn thought he saw a mixture of anger and pity in them as she said slowly, "How was yours?"

In his room—neat, comfortable enough, nothing fancy, Horn noted; about like Mrs. Irwin, you might say—he set his gear on the bed and began unpacking.

When he came to a cigar box fastened with a brass catch—high-class Havanas, those had been, a little dividend left behind when the Spaniards got run out of El Caney, and the box was a good stout one—he paused and set it on the bed.

"How was yours?" the Irwin woman had said. Well, how *had* Tom Horn's life been?

He slid the catch aside and opened the box.

His fingers moved among the contents, raising one object briefly, then dropping it. He knew what was there, and did not have to look at them; but, he did not know why, his fingers moved steadily, lifting, then releasing each item.

A faded picture of a man and woman in front of a

farmhouse, a bunch of kids with them, one with a distant look in his eyes. Another tintype, scratched, of a pretty girl in a gingham dress. A crumbling newspaper engraving of Geronimo. A photo of Sieber in a fancy cardboard frame, standing with one foot on a stuffed bear and grinning foolishly. A round piece of dulled metal with the figure of a man on a bucking horse on one side and the words "World's Champion Cowboy, 1889" engraved on the other.

He swept them back into the box, wondering why he bothered to keep them. He could remember as clearly as he wanted what they stood for, and the things that there weren't any mementos of, too.

He lay on the bed, arms under his head, and looked at the ceiling. Deputy to Bucky O'Neill over in Arizona, some damn good tracking and manhunting under Bucky—dead in Cuba now, poor fellow. The time with the Pinkertons, some good work there, too, getting in with the rustlers until he could take them all in. . . . The Phoenix Fair, where he'd got the goddam fool medal, not knowing then what it had already cost in blood. . . . The war with Spain, and him in charge of all mule transport for the invasion of Cuba—that was high times, and good work done, no doubt about it. He grinned as he remembered the sight of the crazy New Yorker with the spectacles and mustache running up Kettle Hill with a bunch of westerners—some of them men Horn knew—behind him.

That had been a funny business all around, like coming around a circle and meeting yourself again— Lawton was there, screwing up things as usual, a handsome dumb general now instead of a handsome dumb captain; and General Nelson A. Miles, masterminding the whole show as commander in chief. No wonder so much had gone wrong.

"How was yours?". she'd asked him back. He frowned. There didn't seem to be a "how" to his life, come to think of it; it had been him doing things as best he could, knowing that what he did, he did better than anyone—where was the "how" in that?

He sat up and swung his legs over the side of the bed and stared at his image in the mirror over the bureau as if it might give him some answer to the question.

Cold blue eyes, a little lighter than they'd once been, but still seeing as far and clear as ever; tight, closed face; a drooping mustache, grown once when he was courting a woman who had a fancy that way, and not worth the bother of getting rid of after. Nothing remarkable about that face, it seemed to him; it was his face, and that was about it.

He lay back on the bed and put the nagging question out of his mind; no point in keeping at something there wasn't any answer to. The main thing was, as it always was, what came next?

Ed Smalley hurried toward the Irwin Hotel, sourly contemplating the news one of his deputies had just brought him. He was briefly distracted as he passed the smith by the sight of a crowd gathered around a shiny automobile. First one of those in Cheyenne, he thought gloomily, but not the last. Be something *else* it'll turn out to be my job to look after, as if there wasn't enough already. I must of been off my *head* when I run for sheriff.

Mrs. Irwin, rocking on the front porch of her hotel

with her six-year-old daughter in her lap, smiled slightly as she watched the thin young sheriff approach. Poor Ed was always in a fret about something.

"How come you have your hair down, Mama?" Mandy asked.

"More comfortable, this hot weather."

"It makes you look, oh, kind of younger or something."

"No need for that, just for comfort, like I said."

"Ernestina—Ernestina," Smalley called as he loped up to the hotel.

"Hmm?" Mrs. Irwin said, still rocking.

"Did Tom Horn just check in?"

"Um-hmm," she said placidly.

Smalley addressed the child. "Mandy, why don't you go get your mother some water?"

The girl looked at her mother. Mrs. Irwin nodded and said, "Please." Mandy slid from her lap and ran into the hotel. "What's wrong, Ed?" Mrs. Irwin asked.

Smalley paced back and forth on the porch. "Why do you suppose he's been brought here? Must be account of the rustlers . . . damn, what a thing, Tom Horn being brought in to show me up when I'm doing such a great job of keeping the rustlers in line!"

"Oh, Ed," Mrs. Irwin said cheerfully, "you're doing a terrible job. You're a wonderful person, you're just not much of a sheriff.

"Well, *I* know that," Smalley said. "But rustling's just about the biggest business in the state. What can I do alone?" He frowned as he paced half the length of the porch and turned back toward her. "Wonder

166

who brought him in?" He stopped and looked at her. "Something's different about you."

"Yes?" Mrs. Irwin said.

"New dress?"

She looked down at the plain, serviceable garment she always wore on duty, aware, as she had not been for a long time, of Ernestina underneath it. "Sort of."

Mandy returned with a dipper of water. Smalley absently took it from her and drank. "Thanks." He turned to Mrs. Irwin and renewed his complaint. "It's not enough, trying to keep Cheyenne safe all by myself; now I got Tom Horn to contend with!"

"He hasn't done anything yet, Ed," she said soothingly.

Smalley looked bitterly at the hotel, as if he could see through its walls to where the sinister Horn was plotting against the public peace and gloating over the devilment he would bring down on a hardworking sheriff. "He will," he said gloomily.

Horn looked tensely around the small room. Through the paneled door that led out of it he could hear the sound of men talking and laughing. A black man in what looked to Horn a little like a Spanish officer's full-dress uniform hurried past him. "You sure they know I'm here?" Horn called.

Without breaking stride, the liveried servant said, "They're dealing with important matters," and left the room.

Another burst of laughter came to him from the room beyond. If that's how the Wyoming Cattle Club deals with *important matters*, he thought morosely, I bet there's no holding them down when they're having fun.

It was at least twenty minutes later when another servant ushered him through the paneled door and called, "Mr. Horn."

Horn stopped on the threshold and blinked. The room was immense and opulent, brightly lit by an immense chandelier hanging from the center of the ceiling. One wall was taken up by a long bar, tended by yet another black man in livery, and backed by a huge gilt-framed mirror. The other walls displayed portraits of stern, rich-looking men. The subjects of some of the portraits were among the dozen men seated in overstuffed plush chairs placed around the room and looking at him silently. Most held cigars, and the smoke rose in streams in the still air to pool against the ceiling.

Horn cleared his throat. After a moment, one man rose, an impressive figure in a well-cut broadcloth suit; a little fleshy in the face, but with something of the look of the outdoorsman about him. "Mr. Horn, I'm John Noble."

Horn nodded. Noble said, "Brandy?"

"Please."

Noble called to the bartender, "Give Mr. Horn a man's-sized snifter, please." The bartender busied himself with a squat bottle and a bowl-shaped glass that Horn figured would hold about a pint; that would be some drink, all right.

"Come in, sir; let us have a look at you," Noble said. Horn advanced a few paces into the room, looking around in seeming confusion. When the bartender hurried to him with the big glass, Horn was surprised to see that it was only a third filled; but he quickly tasted it, rolling the fiery liquid on his tongue, then took a large swallow.

"You can have a look at us at the same time," Noble went on. "Oh, I know we resemble riffraff—" Horn, the brandy's warmth flooding him, grinned. Anybody who thought these fellows looked like riffraff must not have had much to do with the real article. "—but some of us have fared well enough in life." He pointed around the room. "One of us is an Irish earl, two are in the House of Lords, two are senators, and there is always a state governor or so lurking around somewhere."

Horn nodded and stared uneasily at the floor. 'None of us lives in Cheyenne any more than is necessary, but, you see, we all have one common interest."

"Cattle?" Horn said. He took another gulp from the snifter.

Noble beamed. "Highest marks, sir, excellent. Then you also know our problem."

"Rustlers." Horn drank once more.

"Correct. Our herds are being decimated by rustlers—every man in Wyoming who isn't a shopkeeper is a rustler or a sheepherder, and I do not speak jokngly. We need, very badly, and very quickly, help. And we're prepared to pay top dollar."

"You want a bounty hunter," Horn said.

Several of the club members stirred in their chairs. Noble gave Horn a hard stare. "A bounty hunter, Mr. Horn, is a killer who works outside the law and no one in this room would go near such a person. No, what we are looking for is a first-class stock detective . . . and not all of us are sure you qualify."

169

Horn looked at him silently, then past him to the bartender, and raised his empty glass. The bartender hurried over, carrying the squat bottle, and poured another drink. As he lifted the bottle, Horn raised the glass slightly; the bartender hesitated, then added as much brandy as he had just poured.

Noble waited, distaste evident on his face, until the bartender returned to his station. "Your record is certainly impressive enough," he said. "Obviously we've done some checking on you. A Pinkerton man, very successful, but you left. A marshal, again successful, again you left. Outstanding service in the war with Spain. Many other commendable deeds from your Indian fighting days till now."

Horn nodded. A fair-enough rundown, though it seemed an awfully quick way to handle fifteen years of a man's life. "Then what's the problem?" He drank and waited for the answer.

Noble said, distinctly and evenly, "You drink too much, and we don't know that a drunk can handle our needs."

Horn lowered his eyes and slowly set the brandy glass on the table next to him. The twelve members of the Wyoming Cattle Club looked at him intently; the bartender carefully did not.

"I have been known to down a few, no point in lying," Horn said quietly. "I suppose no one's called me a drunk before." His brief smile drew no response from his audience. "Not to my face anyway."

He looked from still face to still face. "I never yet been hired for something I couldn't do, but . . ." He paused. When he spoke again, his voice had dropped almost to inaudibility. ". . . there's gotta be a first time for everything, I guess. . . ."

Noble's eyes widened as Horn's hand dropped to his waist and came up with a revolver. Horn said dreamily, "I probably couldn't even hit that wall anymore. . . ." The sound of the shot was deafening in the confined room; the slug punched the nail that supported the huge mirror into the wall. The bartender sprang to one side as the mirror slipped to the floor, then slammed forward onto the bar, smashing and scattering glasses and bottles.

The members of the Wyoming Cattle Club sat, stunned, with fear beginning to pinch their features.

The gun danced in Horn's hand as he said, still softly, almost diffidently, "Chances are I could hit the ceiling, if I was close enough. . . ." He whirled and fired again. The club members bolted from their chairs as the chandelier crashed to the floor, and made for the door. They stopped dead when they saw that Horn was covering them with the revolver.

"*Now hear me, you rich bastards!*" he shouted. "I cleaned the rustlers out of northern Colorado and you musta *known* that or you wouldn't have sent for me, so don't bother going on about how am I, or can I uphold your goddam *standards!*" The gun flicked back and forth from one possible target to another. "Hire me, don't hire me, that's up to you, you know where to find me—*but quit blowin' smoke!*" With a tight smile, he said, once again quietly, "I just *know* I could hit the floor."

The gun leaped in his hand. Noble stood frozen-faced as bullets tore up the carpet around his feet.

When the hammer clicked on an empty chamber,

Horn thrust the gun back into his trousers and stormed from the room, through the outer room, where a liveried servant stood pressed against the wall, holding very still, and out onto the street; he slammed the front door hard behind him, setting the brass knocker rattling in brief protest.

There was a saloon across the street, and he broke into a near run as he headed for it. "Leave the bottle," he ordered when the barkeep had poured the first glass of whiskey. The first one steadied him; the second brought him down from his peak of rage, and he allowed himself a grin. Some mess he'd made of that fancy place, all right! Wasn't what Horatio Alger, Jr., would recommend to a worthy lad being interviewed for a job, no doubt about that, but it had sure shaken up those tight-faced cattlemen. And, considering what the job was, the Alger line wouldn't have been all that smart, anyhow. He bet himself a double eagle, even money, that he'd be hearing from Noble again. Next time he went back to that place—if ever—it'd be on different terms, and no sidelong looks at whatever he chose to drink. That brandy, now, that was smooth stuff, went with the rich look of the room. . . .

"Supposed to be very fancy in there."

Startled, wondering if he'd maybe been talking out loud, Horn looked up. A man with a seamed face, on which, Horn thought, he could read a pretty checkered history, was giving him an unpleasant smile, moving up to lean against the bar. "Wyoming Cattle Club, I'm talking about," the man said. Horn looked away from him and drank. "'Course, they don't let us decent folk inside too often."

Another man moved in alongside the first. Both,

Horn saw, as well as the two other men with them, wore holstered revolvers. "You know how those bastards got their money?" the second man said. Horn ignored him and lifted his glass again.

The third man moved to Horn's other side and spoke across him to the first. "So that's Tom Horn, Nickell. I heard about Tom Horn. I thought Tom Horn was eight feet tall."

The fourth man snickered. "I didn't know they piled it that high."

Horn set down his glass and turned, resting his back against the bar. "What do you want me to do?" he said, almost whispering. "Who do you want me to kill?" His eyes scanned the four faces rapidly. "Draw, any of you, all of you. How many of you have to die before there's *quiet?*"

The four faces went slack. Horn estimated that these fellows had taken a worse shock than the men at the Wyoming Cattle Club—by their rules, a lone man being hoorawed by four gun toters just stands there and takes it.

Finally the first one, Nickell, said huskily, "It . . ." He looked around at his companions. "It wouldn't be fair."

"You're right," said the one who had snickered, beginning to edge back. "Four against one—that'd be a helluva thing."

Nickell's eyes were bright with panic as he backed away hastily. "I don't know about you guys," he muttered, "but I don't want it on my conscience."

Horn's lips quirked as he watched them break for the door and vanish through it into the night. That Nickell fellow wouldn't have any conscience to speak of, but he had a prudent regard for his ass. Horn re-filled his glass and settled down to the real business of the night.

Mrs. Irwin pulled a wrapper from the foot of her bed and flung it over her nightgown. She glanced at the clock on the bureau and, in a patch of feeble light from a streetlamp outside, was able to see that it was past eleven.

The crashing noise that had awakened her came again from downstairs. She had a fair idea of what was causing it, and hurried to the top of the stairs.

Horn, she noted, was able to walk fairly steadily, which was remarkable, considering the rich cloud of whiskey aroma that hung about him—he might as well have been bathing in it, she thought—but had considerable trouble navigating. She watched him walk briskly into a wall and rebound, then hurried down and grabbed one of his arms.

"Evening, Mr. Horn," she said quietly.

"It sure is," he said agreeably, looking at her or at least somewhere near her.

She used the arm as a lever to point him at the stairway and start him up the first step. "Enjoying Cheyenne?"

"So far."

She almost stumbled as he took the rest of the stairs in a sudden rush and came to rest against the wall of the second-floor hallway. She went to him and steadied him again, turning him in the direction of his room.

He turned to her. "Hey?"

"Yes?"

"Were you always . . ." He paused and rallied his forces to get it right. "Er-nes-tee-na?"

"Every since I was a baby," she said, shepherding him along the corridor.

"Thass the worst name I ever heard," Horn confided.

"You always had a way with compliments, Mr. Horn," she said calmly.

They were at his door now. He leaned against the wall, breathing heavily, fished in his trouser pocket, brought out the key, and carefully jabbed it against a rose in the corridor's wallpaper. Another try sent the key sliding off the doorknob. She took it from him and unlocked and opened the door.

Horn stumbled inside and fell on the bed, beginning to laugh. The laughter built until he was whooping helplessly.

Mrs. Irwin stood in the doorway, her arms folded. "What?" she asked.

"I just . . ." Horn broke off with a cackle, then started again. "I just challenged four guys to a draw and they all chickened *out.*"

"Why is that funny?"

He looked at her owlishly. "I didn't have any *bullets* in my gun. . . ." He gave a final snort of laughter and rolled over to lie facedown on the bedspread, his eyes already closing.

Mrs. Irwin looked puzzled. "But what if they'd drawn on you?"

"Oh . . ." Horn mumbled drowsily. "*They* wouldn't do *that.* . . ."

She was half smiling as she watched him. She drew her folded arms closer to her body, hugging herself tightly. A rasping snore came from the sleeping man. "Good night, Mr. Horn," she murmured.

But for a long time she did not move from the doorway.

"Uh . . . Mrs. Irwin?"

She opened her eyes and sat up in bed, awake in an instant at the sound of the soft knock at her door and the whisper from the corridor.

"Yes, Mr. Horn?"

"Could I talk to you?"

She pulled the coverlet up to her shoulders and said, "Yes. Come in."

In the dim predawn light, she could see his hair was plastered down, and guessed that he had practically submerged his head in the washbasin on his night-stand; something, anyhow, seemed to have cut down the whiskey aroma.

"That was low," he said from the doorway. "Coming in stinking drunk like that, getting you out of bed. When I woke up just now, it come to me that I shouldn't have done that, put you to that trouble and all." He had moved halfway across the room toward her. "So I come to apologize."

She looked at him gravely. "No, you didn't." Slowly, as if it were a matter of very great moment, and not to be hurried, she drew the sheet and coverlet aside, then held her arms out toward him.

CHAPTER 19

Ernestina looked with some doubt at the plate of food on the table before her. It smelled good, right enough, but it was pretty mixed-up looking, and those bean-sprout things looked awfully like little worms. She didn't really suppose they were, but you heard things about Chinese cooking. . . . It might have been better to have had the chop suey, but it seemed she had that every time she came to Li Ching's. She tried a forkful, and was pleasantly surprised to find that the sprouts were crunchy, not slimy.

Horn came in through the front door and looked around; she waved, and he came to her. "Sorry," he said, sitting across the table from her.

"Did whatever it was go well?" she asked, continuing to eat.

"I got the job, I guess." He picked up a fly-specked menu lying on the table.

"I'm very famous in town these days," she said. "Since we started keeping company."

"That what we're doing?" Horn said. He wondered if Li Ching ever got much call for whatever dung goo gai peen was; a man'd feel like a fool ordering it.

"Do you know how often people look at you?"

Horn, still studying the menu, said, "The guy in the plaid shirt, you mean?"

Ernestina nodded. She said, dropping her voice, "Have you really killed a hundred men? That's what the grocer said today."

"Thousand." Even when they wrote it out in English, it didn't get you much further. What in the hell were cloud ears?

"I was *serious*," she protested.

He looked up at her. "How do you know I wasn't?"

"Why do you talk that way?"

"The more people think I've done, the less I have to do," he said quietly. "The more afraid the better." He looked past her at the restaurant wall and added slowly, "Fear's been good to me."

Ernestina looked at him closely. She opened her mouth to speak, then stopped and looked up. The strange old man in the plaid shirt she had noticed staring at Horn stood beside the table. He was weaving a little on his feet, and fumes of whiskey came from him.

"Always had an eye for faces," he said in a croaking voice. "You're Tom Horn, mustache or not." Horn looked up blankly as the old man held out his hand. "George Crook." Horn's face remained blank. The old man said, "General Crook, remember? Arizona?"

Horn pushed himself up from his seat and said quickly, "Must be not seeing you in uniform that surprised me—you look the same as ever."

Crook grunted. "*I* don't think I do. I get that same reaction a lot." He gave a short bark of laughter. "Everybody thinks I'm dead." He pulled a vacant chair from the next table and sat in it. "Mind if I sit down?"

178

Horn hesitated a moment, then nodded. Crook pulled a brown paper bag from his pocket, with the neck of a flat bottle protruding from it. "Offer you folks a drink? Cuts the gas you get, eating this Chinese stuff."

Ernestina lowered her eyes to her plate. Horn shook his head. Crook grinned, revealing sparse brown teeth, and tilted the bottle to his mouth.

In the early-evening dimness, Horn sat in a rocker on the hotel's front porch. His fingers moved constantly, braiding lengths of cord. Beside him, Crook rocked irregularly. His voice was slurring badly, and Horn wondered if it had been wise to break out another bottle for the old man when his pint was gone. But the poor old bastard seemed to need it.

"Bess move I ever made was leaving the Army," Crook said. "Got my *freedom* now."

Horn continued braiding and, after a while, said, "That's the main thing."

Crook tried to push himself up from the rocker, and nearly pitched forward onto his face. "Got to get on . . . taking the train for Denver in the morning."

"That home now?" Horn asked.

Crook shook his head several times. "*Speaking* 'gagement. Do a lot of that. Schools and such. Talk about the Innian wars. Keeps a man alert, dealing with youngers—youngsters. I guess I got a, a flair for it, that's what they say, anyhow."

"Sounds good," Horn observed, his fingers shuttling cords under and over.

"No it doesn't," Crook said, a little more clearly.

Horn looked at him. "You can tell I'm just bullshitting, can't you?"

Horn nodded. "I guess."

"It just makes me so damn mad . . ." Crook was silent awhile, then said, "I was gonna feel sorry for myself . . ." He stopped again, then went on. "What's wrong with that, no one else is left to do it for me. I'm all I've got. But what gets me is Lawton's a general and Miles almost got nominated for President, and I'm lying to kids for a living."

He managed to get out of the rocker, and walked cautiously down the porch stairs. "I didn't mean to be here when I was sixty," he said; whether to himself or Horn, Horn could not tell.

The little man gave a limp gesture that might have been a wave and walked down the darkening street.

Horn chewed slowly on the chunk of raw bacon he held as he hunkered by the trail. The twenty head of cattle he had seen two hills away came into view again, being expertly herded by three men. He made no effort to hide or to move out of the way as the cattle came on. He knew when the men spotted him by an abrupt tensing of their bodies.

They came on slowly, eying him. As they reached him, he stood and jerked his head toward the cattle. "Yours?"

The leader nodded. Horn asked, "Mavericks?"

The man in the lead said, "Just unbranded strays is all."

Horn moved among the cattle. "Hey? . . . This one's got a J Bar N brand. . . . So's this one. Isn't that John Noble's? Coulda sworn it was. . . ." He was deep in the midst of the animals now; one of the rustlers stepped behind him.

"They're *all* J Bar N," Horn said, in the tone of one passing on a curious item of news. He whirled as the hand of the man behind him slid toward a holstered gun. "*Don't even think about it!*" His own gun was out and he was away from the cattle and covering all three of them.

The rustlers exchanged glances. One broke into a low chuckle; the others joined him. Horn looked at them. "You're going to stand trial for rustling, why's that funny?"

"Well," the oldest one said, "we're the Laughoff brothers, see? I'm Art, them's Vern and Gene. And it's like they say, Laughoff by name, Laughoff by nature. It comes natural to us."

He saw the joke a couple of weeks later in the Cheyenne courtroom, when the judge's gavel came down and the judge's voice said, "Not guilty."

Horn glared at the complacent judge, the cheerful jury, and the grinning Laughoffs.

"Insufficient evidence," the judge went on. "Case dismissed, court's adjourned." He gaveled his desk once again, rose, and started to leave the courtroom.

Horn rose in his place and called after him, "What the hell's *sufficient* evidence? I caught 'em in the *act!*"

The courtroom door closed, and the judge was gone. Vern Laughoff waved derisively at Horn.

"Well, at last you see our situation," Noble said. Horn sat hunched morosely over the long bar at the Wyoming Cattle Club. A smaller chandelier hung from the ceiling now, and the gilt frame—but not the mirror—hung once more behind the bar. Noble, not making a point of it, had said that a new one had been ordered made up in San Francisco.

"No one likes a rich man," Noble, standing beside him at the bar, went on. "The juries are either poor people or other rustlers. Convictions are hard to come by." He reached for the bottle of brandy that stood on the bar and poured it into Horn's glass. "You like this, take a couple bottles with you."

"You're a generous man, Mr. Noble," Horn said dryly.

"Ice in the winter is what I give away, Mr. Horn." Noble bent until his head was almost touching Horn's and spoke quietly. "I'm not saying to you now what I'm saying to you, you understand? Because I'm a lawyer and I love and respect the law. The same for the senators and governors here in the Wyoming Cattle Club. We all got where we are by using the law, not breaking it."

Horn was not impressed by this tribute to the grandeur of legality. It had the ring of a funeral service for its subject. "Finish it," he said.

"When you said that first night what we wanted was a bounty hunter?" Noble said. Horn nodded. "You were right. I started you off as a stock detective to show you we couldn't win by working within the law."

"I knew that." Horn took another sip of the brandy, watching Noble from the corner of his eyes.

"Well, you better know *this*—you ever say you were hired by me as a bounty hunter, I'll lie all the way to the grave."

"You got my word, Mr. Noble," Horn said. Noble did not speak for a second, and Horn added, very gently, "I don't give it every day."

Noble nodded slowly. Horn looked around the room. With just him and Noble in it, it seemed even richer than it had before, with no people to distract the eye from its appointments. "Seven hundred dollars a rustler," Noble said.

Horn looked at the brandy glass. "That's top dollar, all right."

"That could be just the start. There's a lot of members who could be *very* grateful to someone who stopped the rustling. You know where Utah, Wyoming, and Colorado come together?"

Horn nodded. "Brown's Hole."

"Fifty square miles of killers and thieves," Noble said heavily. "A man could make important friends by cleaning out Brown's Hole now. . . ."

He and Horn exchanged tight smiles as they lifted their glasses and drank. Horn was already working it out. The seven hundred a head was good only if it wasn't claimed too often. Grateful senators and governors and such couldn't do much for a man who raised too much dust, made it too clear what was going on. The thing was to make each seven-hundred-dollar kill do some extra work for him.

As he had told Ernestina Irwin, fear had been good to him.

CHAPTER 20

Horn had no interest in the ages-long working of geological forces that had formed Brown's Hole: the beds of ancient seas that had dried out, been turned to stone by heat and pressure, lifted high above their old level by the slow movement of the earth's crust, then scoured by wind and weather and the patient workings of a network of streams and rivers of which the puny descendants, the Green and the Bear, still flowed into a maze of canyons and box canyons, hills, mountains, and wind-carved rock formations.

Two things only about Brown's Hole concerned him at the moment: the fact that its makeup provided an ideal haven for a small army of rustlers who could melt into any of a thousand refuges in the rocky hills and yet find pasturage for their stolen herds in the lush valley of the Green; and that, right now, it was damnably cold, with a harsh wind biting through his clothing and into his body.

The weather did not concern him much. He knew from long experience how much worse it would be before he would have to stop functioning; how he felt while he was functioning was not important.

From his vantage point high on the slope of one of

the Uinta Mountains, he could see down into the river valley, and into several of the rocky gorges that opened onto it. From time to time there was movement, of animals and men, and he noted those movements carefully. As he watched, crouching, he braided cord together, making another lariat.

With dusk, the wind rose and the temperature dropped. He waited until lights glowed dimly in several of the crude cabins the rustlers had constructed, and marked their location in his mind.

He did not move down toward the cabins that night, but sheltered in the hills, content to wait until his reconnaissance was complete and perfect. As he composed himself for sleep on the rocky ground, his thoughts turned back to the chase after Geronimo. There wasn't much left of it in his mind except the memory of searing heat, endless days and weeks of it. This would be a change, anyhow. Heat and cold, there wasn't that much to choose between them. Either could kill you or slow you dangerously if you didn't know what you were doing. . . .

Briefly, when sleep was slow in coming, he considered the job ahead. It was a good thing Cassidy and the Wild Bunch weren't holed up here just now. Cassidy could be too much of a wild card in this game. Without him, it would be pretty much straight draw poker, with Horn stacking the deck.

He turned on his side, feeling sleep beginning to come to him. Be nice, he thought drowsily, if Ernestina was here. Damn fool name, but a fine woman, in bed and out . . . .

The next day he spent in further scouting. Toward

dusk, satisfied, he made his way down the well-hidden trail that led to one of the cabins.

The big man, half a head taller than six feet and broad to match, sat in the tiny cabin, clumsily stitching together a bridle that had worn through. A kerosene lantern cast a dim light over the work; he thought vaguely of cleaning the smudged glass of the chimney, but decided against it. Too hot now, it would probably break if he handled it, and it would be a full day's ride out and back to get another one.

He jabbed the saddler's needle into his finger and yelped as a voice came to him through the cabin's single window:

"You've got sixty days."

The giant rustler dropped the pieces of bridle and stared into the chill darkness. "Whoozat?"

"Eight weeks," the voice said mournfully, "and I'm coming back. If you're still here, you die."

"Who is it?" the rustler called. His hands slid slowly toward the rifle on the table in front of him.

"*Don't*," the voice said. "*I could kill you now!*" There was a loud report from the darkness and splinters sprang from the wall planking inches from the rustler's head. "See?" The rustler nodded.

He squinted into the darkness but could see only the back hole of the window. "Who . . . are . . . you?" he called. He sat numbly staring at the empty window, listening to the wail of the rising wind.

Horn, eyes wide and staring, drove his lathered horse through the early-morning light toward where a bewildered-looking young man stood in front of a cabin. He pulled up the horse and seemed almost to fall from the saddle. "Water?" he said in a trembling voice. "You got enough to spare?"

"What's the matter?" the young rustler asked.

"Oh, *Christ*," Horn said, "but I never had no experience like that!" He held out his hand; it trembled in the younger man's grip. "Name's Frank Hicks and I had a place twenty miles downriver, and—oh, my God . . ."

"Go on," the young rustler said.

"This voice come in the night—a spook—and it said, 'You're a dead man, Frank Hicks, you stick in Brown's Hole.' And I couldn't see nothin', but this voice went *on* about what was gonna happen to me if I stayed. . . ."

"What would happen?" the young rustler asked uneasily.

Horn let his eyes widen even farther and did what he could to make his lower lip quiver. "Indian torture," he said hollowly.

The young rustler looked at him with uncertainty growing on his face. "There's no Indians . . . ."

Horn closed his eyes and shook his head. "There's *always* Indians." He pointed up into the mountains. "Maybe waiting up there this minute . . . waiting to reclaim their land." He let the rustler ponder this for a moment while he stepped to the water butt and filled his canteen. "What they get up to," he murmured, with the fixed stare of one who is reliving terrible scenes, "you wouldn't believe. What they cut off you and what they do with what they cut off, I don't like to say." He screwed the cap back onto the canteen. "Thanks," he said more briskly, and scrambled onto his horse.

"Good luck!" he called back to the young rustler. "You got more guts'n me . . . ."

The rustler looked after him until he was lost to sight, and did not move. At a sound behind him, he cried out and whirled, reaching for the gun at his waist. A tin can, overturned by the wind, rolled lazily in a half circle. The rustler stared around, suddenly aware of how very close the trees were to his cabin, and of what they might hide.

"You want to die, it's *easy* . . ." the voice floated into the darkened cabin on the night wind. The man on the cot, not much more than a boy, shivered and pulled the blankets closer around him. It was scarcely above freezing, but sweat stood out on his forehead.

". . . just stay where you are the next eight weeks. You do that, you're dead."

The three men in the large cabin—one immensely fat, one thin as a rail, one short as a jockey—had their hands in the air, but seemed more angered than frightened by the eerie voice.

". . . you're dead . . ."

"I heard that voice before," Art Laughoff muttered. Vern and Gene nodded; the other five men at the food-laden table looked bewildered.

"Sumbitch is tryin' to spook us, that's—" Gene began.

"Unless any of you wants to die now . . . ." A rifle slug from the dark shattered a plate on the table.

"Who wants to die *now* . . . ?" The heavy earthenware platter of stew exploded, showering the eight with shards of china and gobbets of meat.

"Just raise your hand . . . ."

The eight men sat in deathly silence and immobility after the voice faded and was replaced by the keening of the wind.

At dawn, Horn rode out of Brown's Hole. Looking back as he ascended the steep trail, he could see a good deal of movement from cabin to cabin, knots of men talking and gesticulating. He smiled once and turned away. The wicked flee where no man pursueth, the Bible said; but it didn't hurt a bit to give them an extra incentive.

"Who's my rival?" Ernestina said. Horn looked up from his task of sewing a button on his shirt—Ernestina would have done that, but he knew he had a way of getting it on tighter and neater than most women could manage—and admired the way she looked, lounging in his bed. A lot younger in the lamplight than in daylight, and any age you could want when the lamp was out. She was rummaging through the old cigar box, and now held up the yellowed picture of the good-looking girl in the gingham dress.

Horn gave the photograph a quick glance. "Aw, wasn't she pretty? When I was that age, I left Missouri and we were in love and my last night I whispered, 'Wait for me,' and she said, 'Nope,' and I said, 'Huh?' and she said, 'You're not the kind that's ever coming home, I'm not growing old for you, Tom Horn'."

He returned to his sewing. "You know, she was right. I can't even remember her name."

Ernestina returned the photograph to the box and

began turning over its other contents. "What do you think would have happened if I'd stayed in Arizona?"

Horn sent the needle through one of the holes in the button and the fabric beneath. "We'd have made love a lot—"

"Good."

"—then probably I would have gotten you all nice and pregnant. And after that I'd have run out on you."

"Not so good." She pulled out a badge with a frayed blue ribbon attached to it. "What's this 'World's Champion Cowboy' thing?"

Horn pulled the thread tight and bit it off close to the firmly attached button. "Nothing."

"You really won it?" Ernestina said. "Wasn't it hard?"

Horn's face was suddenly bleak. "*Nothing's hard for me,*" he said harshly.

Ernestina pressed back against the pillow in a fleeting gesture of fear. "Well, that's not my fault," she said defensively.

Horn looked at her, sighed, and spoke more gently. "I didn't even want to enter the damn contest. I was due to take the Apache Kid and some others to jail. But the head marshal said, 'No, we'll do the escorting, you enter,' so I did and I won."

He grimaced and grabbed at the whiskey bottle on the table next to him and took a long drink. His eyes were half closed and his voice thinner as he went on: "And my marshal, and the others, they all but one got murdered on the way and the Kid escaped. What happened was the Indians planned the escape while they were being taken along . . . none of the whites spoke Apache."

He reached for his rifle leaning against the wall, and began stripping it down. Gun oil, cloth swabs, and a cleaning rod were laid out on the table next to the bottle.

"I found this out just before they handed me that medal, Ernestina . . . four men gone and me with a medal in my hands. I started drinking bad and this guy came up to me and asked would I do my act in Europe. It was Buffalo Bill himself, Colonel William Frederick)goddam) Cody, and I said, 'My *act*?' and he said, 'That's right, for my Wild West Show,' and I started screaming, 'I don't do no goddam *act*, everybody's *dead*!' " He looked again at the badge, and said quietly, "So when I said that this was nothing, well, that's all it was . . . ."

She looked at his hands expertly moving over the weapon, cleaning it, reassembling it. She remembered the feel of his hands . . . they were good at anything they did. "Leaving tonight?" she said. Horn nodded. "How long?" Horn shrugged. "But you'll be careful, you'll come back."

"You can't hurt a Christian," Horn said.

She looked at him as always at times like this, unhappy to have to admit that she was memorizing him . . . as if she might have to depend on memory. "You never like talking about the past. Why is that?"

"The past has always been rough country, Ernestina." He shook some rifle cartridges out of a cardboard box and hefted them absently in his hand. "And I didn't mean to be here when I was forty."

CHAPTER 21

Horn walked toward the darkened cabin, no more than minimally cautious in his approach. Even in the dimness of evening, it had the look of a place that hadn't been lived in for a while . . . eight weeks, say.

He opened the door and looked inside the single room. There were a few clumsily built sticks of furniture, but everything worth carrying away was gone, and there was untracked dust on the floor.

His teeth gleamed briefly in the dusk. The Indian torture story, with the right audience, worked wonders. He calculated that the young rustler hadn't stayed around past noon of the day Horn had ridden up to him faking panic.

He whistled shrilly once, and his horse came to him.

Two miles farther along he found another deserted cabin. That would, he recalled, be the one where the occupant had just stayed in bed and shivered while Horn warned him from the night. Maybe he'd have joined forces with the other fellow now, the two of them looking for work a little easier on the nerves than rustling, far away from where there were any Indians. They could be in San Francisco or New York by now, clerking in some store and thankful to be alive . . . .

Horn reviewed his mental list of the rustlers and their locations. The *next* place wasn't likely to be abandoned.

The giant rustler sat where he had been two months before. He was not repairing his bridle now, but merely sitting quietly, as if waiting for something. His hands lay in his lap.

From the darkness came the voice he had heard eight weeks before: "It's sixty da—"

The rustler whirled, whipping up the shotgun that had been concealed beneath the table's oilcloth cover, blasted through the window with one barrel, then the second. As the echoes of the shots died away, he jabbed the lamp out with his gun butt and, in the sudden darkness, slammed two more shells into the weapon's breech.

He stood, trying to still his ragged, harsh breathing, listening intently. For a moment, there was no sound; then a bubbling, agonized cry came to him: *"Christ-o-mighty . . ."* Silence fell again.

The rustler snarled and shook his head, eased the shotgun out the window and fired twice again, then reloaded. "You're out there," he called. "I know you're out there . . . *you didn't fall!"*

"No fooling you, is there?" the voice said cheerfully. The rustler fired again.

Through what remained of the night, he peered uselessly into the darkness, firing from time to time at where the mocking voice, ever-shifting location, taunted him.

At first light, he busied himself as if for a siege,

slamming a rough shutter over the window and bolting it, pushing the heavy bed against the door, piling chairs and the table, even a heavy skillet, on the bed. It wouldn't stop anybody long, but long enough . . . .

He moved the one chair he had not used for the barricade to a corner of the room and stood on it. He slid a catch aside, and a hinged square of the ceiling swung down. He swiftly patted the two pistols jammed into his belt, checking their presence, reached up, and hoisted himself through the opening.

He sprawled on the shallowly pitched roof and, even before getting to his feet, grabbed his weapons. In a half crouch, he peered toward the woods from where the voice had come all through the night—

"Behind you."

The rustler whirled, bringing both guns to bear on the man who stood barefoot on the roof. Before he could fire, the man's gun boomed, sending him off the roof in a neat backward dive; he hit the ground solidly, but was past being injured by the fall.

Horn grunted as he vaulted from the roof, letting bent knees take up the force of the drop. He bent down and picked up a rounded rock about the size of his fist, and went to where the dead rustler stared sightlessly at the lightening sky. He took a handful of the man's hair, lifted the lolling head, and slipped the rock under it.

The rustler looked as though he were peering hard at his boot tops and not caring for what he saw.

The kerosene lamps flung distorted shadows on the wall as the three men paced the cabin agitatedly.

"I'm not gonna tell you again," the painfully thin rustler said, "it ain't gonna be me."

"It's gotta be," the obese one shouted.

"You're the fastest," the diminutive one pointed out. "You'd do it best."

"No and that's it!"

The fat one held up three canteens; they clanked together with a hollow sound. "We need water and the river's just outside. Who do *you* think oughta go?"

The skinny one looked at him sourly. "He's gonna kill whoever goes, so I don't much care if it isn't me."

"You're crazy," the short one put in. "I don't even think he's out there, I think he's gone. He trapped us in here this morning, sure, but we outlasted him."

The skinny rustler jerked his head toward the front of the cabin. "Stand in the doorway, then."

"If I stand in the doorway, will you fill the canteens?"

The skinny one nodded. "I will." The short man licked his lips and looked around. His two companions regarded him with a kind of respectful mournfulness, as if turning over in their heads what would be the nicest things they could say about him after he was dead.

He walked to the front door and held his hand poised over the bolt. Carefully, he eased it to one side until only the pressure of his hand held the door shut.

A brief blast of cold air invaded the room as he whipped the door open, then slammed it and slid the bolt home. "There," he said proudly, looking toward his thin colleague.

The skinny rustler shook his head. "I'm not going."

The small man slammed his fist on the table. "I just

risked my *life*, you can't change your goddam mind—"

"You didn't risk nothin', you did it so quick—"

The fat rustler groaned. "Jesus, *I'll* do it." He strode to the door and flung it open. He stood there, filling the doorway, for a moment. The other two edged away to the corners of the room, out of any likely line of fire. The man at the door stepped back and slammed and bolted it again, and turned to face the two others. The three stared at each other for a long time, and finally the thin rustler said resignedly, "Gimme the goddam canteens." The small man handed them over. "Open the goddam door." Standing to one side, the fat rustler did so.

The skinny man walked briskly out into the night. Ahead, he could see the gleam of moonlight on the river. There was a sound—a snapping twig?—to his left, and he spun and cried, "Whozere?"

There was no reply, and no repetition of the noise, and he relaxed a little. As he approached the river, he began to move faster. A bird cry came from the same direction as the first sound. He broke into a run, muttering, "Jesus . . . Jesus . . . Jesus . . . ." He kept up this litany as he reached the river, knelt, and submerged the canteens in it, let them gurgle full, capped them, regained his feet, and ran full tilt back toward the cabin. As he neared it, he began shouting, "Open it! *Open it!*" Just as it seemed that he would crash into the door, it was flung wide, and he catapulted inside, letting the canteens drop and fetching up against the far wall.

With the door slammed and bolted once more, the three looked at each other in silence for a few seconds, then the skinny one whooped, "I did it!" And the others were shouting, "You did it!" and pounding him on the back. . . .

Wood splintered as the boards covering the window were shattered by a figure hurtling into the room, two guns out and firing, battering their ears with a sudden horrible thunder.

When the room, stinking of burned powder, was silent again, the three lay sprawled on the floor. The fat one stirred and sat up. "Where you hit?" he managed to croak to the small rustler.

"In the . . . in the . . . ." He patted himself tentatively. "I coulda swore he got me in the chest. . . ." He sat up. "Where you hit?"

"I think . . . he missed me," the fat man said, after a quick inspection.

The skinny rustler now sat up. "He missed me, too!" He began to laugh.

"He missed us all!" the fat man crowed. "He ain't no better shot than that, what was we *scared* of?" The three roared with contemptuous laughter and rolled on the floor.

The fat man, feeling a sudden damp chill under his meaty shoulders, sat up suddenly. His laughter died away as he saw the three canteens, riddled with holes and empty of water, and the widening pool around them. The other two followed his gaze and fell silent.

They sat on the floor, staring at each other and shivering. There was no sound but that of the wind outside.

Vern Laughoff stood by the barely open door and peered out into the gray light of late afternoon. "Goddammit, Art, we should go now while we can see—we'll cover each other."

His eldest brother looked around the well-built cabin, the neat stack of arms against the wall, and the alert, tough men lounging on chairs and cots, arms against the wall, and said impatiently, "There's eight of us, for chrissakes, quit talking running."

Vern turned from the door. "I don't care how many we got, you know how many're *dead*? Half Brown's Hole's murdered and the other half's run off."

Gene Laughoff spoke up. "I think it's a gang. A gang of goddam Indians."

"It's gotta be Horn," Art said. "He's part Indian, everybody says so. And I still say it was his voice we heard that time." He glanced at the door, out of which Vern was looking once more.

"Think he's out there?" Vern said.

"Somewhere."

Vern scanned the sky. "Gonna snow."

"Good," Art said, moving to the door and reaching past Vern to pull it shut. "Let him freeze his ass off!"

Snow did fall in the night. It lay lightly on the figure curled around the tiny fire far up the mountainside. Horn lay still, relaxing, willing himself not to waste body heat by shivering. The Indian-style fire was enough to keep him alive, and that was what counted, not whether he was comfortable.

Vern Laughoff looked out the cabin door. A thin layer of fresh snow lay across the open ground between the building and the trees. The early sun did not reach down this far, and was just catching trees and rock at the rim of the gorge that held the cabin, but it was light enough for him to see that the snow was smooth, with no marks of a prowler's footprints. He was considering checking the snow at the rear of the cabin when his youngest brother, Gene, stirred on his cot in the corner, yawned, and sat up.

"Watcha cooking?" he said sleepily.

"Cooking? I'm not—" Vern sniffed. Wood smoke. And the potbelly stove was cold and empty . . . . "Art! Art!"

Art Laughoff rolled up on one elbow.

"He's burning us out!"

Gene and the five other rustlers were awake in an instant and scrambling from their cots. Art was already on his feet—like the others, he had slept fully dressed against the cold—and buckling on his gunbelt. "Get the horses, bring 'em here!"

Vern started through the door. Art called to him impatiently, "Not alone, for chrissakes!" and shoved three of the others after him, noting that they all had guns.

He pulled on his boots and ran to a corner of the room. The smoke smell was stronger now, and he could hear a crackling from above. Hastily he scooped up a bundle of greenbacks and stuffed them into a sack, then a pouch of gold pieces. Art set to filling another sack; the two other rustlers came over to help them.

Probably what the bastard's figuring on, Art thought—drive us out and loot the place. Well, it ain't gonna work. Too many of us for him to take on, and we ain't about to be scared off, like them others . . . .

The shots came in a single burst of sound, too fast to count.

Art Laughoff dropped his sack and ran to the door. "Vern?" Only the wind answered. "*Vern?*"

He gestured to Gene and the two other men. They reached for their gun belts, checked their revolvers for loads, and followed him through the door.

They ran around the corner of the cabin, boots crunching in the new snow, and stopped. Vern Laughoff and the three men who had gone out with him were lying face-up in the snow. The head of each was propped at a curious angle by a fist-sized rock.

They looked beyond the bodies and, for a moment, did not move.

Horn squatted on his haunches five yards away. He was not looking at them, but was intent on his swiftly moving fingers, braiding cord together.

A long career as a rustler had accustomed Art Laughoff to gunplay. The six-gun was a tool of his trade, and he was as good with it as he had had to be. There were a few stubborn cowboys who had raised persistent objections to his appropriation of their employers' property, and a couple of stock detectives and Pinkertons, who were now huddles of bones in remote places unless someone had bothered to hunt them out and bury them, to bear mute witness to that. He and Vern and Gene had stood off a posse once, in a fight that lasted most of a day, cutting the ten men down to four and not taking a scratch. He despised the quick-on-the-draw gunmen who seemed to make a career of quarreling and shooting people, making a game out of what was a serious business; but he had made sure that he was as good as any of them, and had, when he had had to, downed his share of them.

But he had never faced anything like this. The indifferent figure, squatting beyond the bodies of his brother and his three friends, silent in the morning stillness, only the fingers moving as they slipped cord over cord, cord between cord, steadily lengthening the braid . . . that was no way even *human*, he told himself, panic starting to rise in him. That was old Death himself, just waiting. . . .

He looked up once to where sunlight caught a canyon rim and a lone pine; it seemed to him that he could see every needle on every branch. It would be a good thing to go up to that tree and lie under it and watch clouds for a while.

He sighed and grabbed for his revolver; it was out and firing in a split second; so were Gene's and those of the two men siding him.

Horn's guns danced and spun in the early light, each jerking to a quick burst, Gatling-fast.

When the echoes died away, he reached behind him for the four rocks he had waiting there.

Riding up the trail as he had eight weeks before, Horn looked back into Brown's Hole. The cabins were still there, except for the smoldering ruin of the Laughoffs' place. But there were no knots of anxious men, running back and forth and conferring. Nothing moved except the trees bending to the wind.

The cabins would have other tenants in time. But not for quite some time. And, whenever and whoever they were, they wouldn't sleep easily at night.

* * *

The Wyoming Cattle Club was again deserted except for Horn and Noble. That suited Horn. He had no ambition to hang around with earls and senators—no ambition, it struck him, for much of anything, except to do what came along. But for Tom Horn, there'd always be something coming along. He sipped at the brandy and considered that he might develop a taste for the stuff. It hit some different than whiskey did, so you could get drunk with a little variety.

"Some of the members were chary of accepting your count, Mr. Horn," Noble said, "but I persuaded them that, as you indicated at our first meeting, you were a man of your word."

"You also done some pretty close checking," Horn observed. "What I hear, some of those fellows from Brown's Hole are now punching cows for the J Bar N, all reformed and respectable, and answering a lot of questions from the boss."

Noble shrugged. "If they're on the loose, they'll be a thorn in my side; and they'll know better than most how to guard my stock against rustlers. And of course I've had a few talks with them about their . . . experiences. And yes, they do verify what you've said, all except for the Laughoff gang."

"Which they couldn't, seeing as the Laughoffs was the last ones there, and ain't nobody likely to be running tours into the Hole to view the remains."

"We'll take the Laughoffs on your say-so, though I must say that eight rustlers at seven hundred dollars amounts to quite a bit of money."

Horn gave him a sidewise look. "You want a discount for quantity, Mr. Noble, go buy dry goods."

Noble grinned. "What was all that business about the stones for? Seems kind of a waste of time."

Horn stared into his glass. "I figure them stones saved a lot of fellows' lives, you know? Kind of like a sign to men I'm after who's on their trail. Like in Brown's Hole, a bunch of 'em'll get spooked and cut out, they see that stone. Save me the trouble of dealing with 'em permanent." He drank from the glass. "Save the Wyoming Cattle Club considerable seven-hundred-dollar payments, too."

Noble studied him for a moment. "All right, Mr. Horn, it's done and you've banked the money. And I mean it's *done*. You understand me—it never happened, and it's not going to happen again. If you want regular work as a stock detective, working within the law, we'll be prepared to consider taking you on on normal terms. But the bounty business, and stones under the head . . . that's over."

Horn looked at both of them in the finally arrived replacement mirror, the fleshy, imposing cattleman, the battered-looking fellow with the drooping mustache and tired eyes. "Sure is, Mr. Noble," he said slowly. "I don't do that for fun."

The boy paused on his way to the corral, holding the heavy water bucket. He wondered if he had heard a noise off to his right. Something crunching on the frozen ground? He decided after a moment that it had only been the bare branches of the stand of cottonwoods scraping in the light wind. He'd better tell Pa about it when he got back to the house, though. Pa was edgy about everything these days, ever since the word had gone out that it was best to lay off stock from the big owners. The boy considered that Pa hadn't been over-smart in rustling those three head from Burton's place—too close by, and Burton wasn't the man to be taken in by some fancy work on a brand with a running iron; he'd done enough of that himself—but Pa wasn't about to take advice from a kid. Maybe in a couple of years, when he was fifteen or so, and working with Pa, he'd be able to get a word in about what he thought—

His hat flew off as his head jerked with the shock of the rifle slug that punched into his shoulder blade. He was aware of a loud noise, then another; and something hit him hard, low in the back. He started to see the ground coming toward him, but both vision and thought ended before he slammed limply onto it.

"Willie?"

There was no answer. Kels Nickell burst from the small frame house and ran toward where the boy lay. When he was ten yards away, he heard a sharp report and felt a burning along one arm, like a branding iron briefly laid on it. He glared toward the stand of trees, standing still for a moment; then more shots sent clods of frozen dirt showering a yard or so from him. He turned and ran back toward the house, calling, "Willie—somebody got Willie!"

His wife's face was pinched and her eyes were wide as she burst from the front door. "Willie got shot!" she wailed.

Nickell started to wave her back as she ran toward him, then realized that there was no more rifle fire coming from the trees; he turned and went with her toward where their son lay.

A few feet away, they stopped. Willie stared at them sightlessly, his head propped by a rock the size of a man's fist.

CHAPTER 22

Horn and Ernestina walked slowly along the street,
not really stopping to inspect the windows of the
shops, but enjoying what they saw there. Ernestina
gave passing admiration to a display of what pur-
ported to be French bonnets; Horn was taken by a
selection of gramophones. He noticed that a couple of
them were a new model, using flat discs instead of the
usual cylinders. Might be a nice thing to get one of
them for Ernestina; she'd like it for Mandy, anyhow,
only probably the kid would spend all day listening to
it, never get outside or read a book. The thing about
gadgets, you could get caught up with them too easy
and not pay any mind to what counted. But it was
good to know that if he fancied one of the things, and
Ernestina okayed it, there was a balance in the bank
to pay for it, or just about anything else he took a
mind to buy. Never had been much reason to want to
buy stuff before, but . . . keeping company, call it
that . . . with Ernestina, that made things different.
He could sense that he was circling around something,
coming closer to it, the way a hawk moves in ever-
narrowing turns, and that, pretty soon, he might just
drop down out of the big sky onto something he

wanted—turning Ernestina from *a* woman into *his* woman. He wasn't sure he wanted that, but that was the way things were shaping. He felt the warm pressure of her side as her arm crooked in his—she wasn't wearing stays anymore, ever since he'd told her he didn't care to peel a woman like a prickly pear.

She stopped and called behind her, "Mandy!" She waited, looking back, and called again, "Mandy, catch up, *I mean it*."

The girl darted out from an alleyway a few yards back, and darted toward them. Ernestina turned to Horn and said quietly, "Ever since Willie Nickell died, I get scared if I let her out of my sight."

Horn nodded. There'd been some foofaraw about that, then suddenly a lot of quiet. He wondered what kind of asshole would backshoot a thirteen-year-old kid. Someone who liked to hurt without any risk to his own skin; there were enough of those, around Cheyenne, or any place.

"Friend Tom."

Horn turned to watch the rider approaching him up the street. White teeth gleamed in the lean, dark face under the neat mustache; the rider, short and fleshier than when he'd last seen him, wore a flat white straw hat, distinctly out of place in the still-chilly Cheyenne spring.

"Friend Tom, 'tis I," the man called out cheerfully.

"Who is that?" Ernestina asked.

"Joe Lefors," Horn muttered. "U.S. marshal some damn place now, I think. When he was young, he was the best. We drink and lie to each other a lot—he thinks he can hold more than me." Lefors rode up to them and stopped, looking down with a wide smile. "Joe."

"I am here to apply my skills to the Nickell case," Lefors announced.

"Then," Horn said solemnly, "I guess it will remain forever unsolved."

Lefors burst into brief laughter. He fished a watch from his vest pocket and studied it. "I'm staying at the Inter Ocean. Give me an hour, and then consider yourself challenged to a return drinking bout. Wasn't for a touch of the ague, I'd have had you under the table last time, down in Deadwood."

"Loser buys all liquor?" Horn asked.

"Naturally." Lefors' smile widened as he lifted the straw skimmer from his head and bowed slightly in the saddle in Ernestina's direction. "And thank you for introducing me to your lady friend. I can tell your manners have greatly improved."

Horn looked after him as he rode down the street, wondering why Lefors was still laughing.

Ernestina looked at him. He waited for what she was going to say, what she'd have to say: "Tom, do you think you should . . . ?" "Tom, do you have to . . . ?" "Tom, why don't you . . . ?"

She said, "I'll see you when you get back."

"You was there when Bucky O'Neil got it?" Lefors asked.

"Not *there*," Horn said carefully, lifting his glass. "Woon't wanta fool ya, though I could make the claim and you none the wiser. In Cuba, yes; right where poor Bucky fell, no. But they told me about it, the fellows that was. I wanned to see him, me havin' been his deputy back in Arizona, but by the time I got there, no soap. They tole him, 'Bucky, keep your head down,' but he says, 'There ain't no Spanish bullet goin' to get me,' and stood up. An' next, blip!—down he goes, shot clean through the head. I guess," Horn sighed, taking another gulp of the whiskey, "if he'd of remembered the Spaniards was using Mausers, which is of your German manufac-ture, he would of been more careful, 'cause, come to it, Bucky was right, wasn't no Spanish bullet got him, but a Dutch one. So what he said was true, much good it done him."

"The way I hear it, you could of stayed with the Army," Lefors said. He was tilted back in his chair, his straw hat canted forward, shading his eyes.

"I worked in a civilian cap-a-city once for General Nelson A. Miles before then," Horn said, "and I didn't cotton to the experience. A war on, and something happening that's one thing, everybody pitches in. But withouten no war, you got to figure you're in an outfit that Nelson A. Piles is commander in chief of and that furthermore turns Henry W. Lawton into a general, which ain't no place for a man that's got any kind of opinion of hisself to be." He peered at Lefors. "Hey, drink up." Lefors tilted the glass to his lips. "Now, was I an insurance agent, I'd charge ten prices to sell a policy to anybody serving under Lawton. You know what that fool done in Cuba? He sent his men ashore at Daiquiri right under emplacements up on the hills there. Wasn't that the Spaniards was as much fools as Lawton and run off before he got there, wasn't a man as'd got off the beach." He poured from the bottle that stood on the table between them.

"Hot in here," he said. "You wanna open the door

some more?" Lefors glanced toward the door to the room, which stood barely ajar. "Window's better," he said, and went to one, shoving the sash up.

"Biggest thing ever happened to you was getting Geronimo, wasn't it?" Lefors said, taking his seat again and touching his glass to his lips.

"I *tole* you about that a dozen times," Horn said, grinning and taking a gulp of whiskey. "You want the time where we fought knife to knife, or the time he had me by the hair, was just about to scalp me, lifted me off the ground, eight feet tall, he was, and I turned and bit his nose off? Lissen," he said heavily, slamming the palm of his hand on the table—harder than he'd meant to; it stung—"yeah, I got Geronimo, I tracked him across purgatory, hell, and Texas, not much difference between 'em, and I got my man. Don't hear as you're doin' too well in that line."

Lefors' lips thinned. "Cassidy and Sundance, you mean?" Horn nodded, grinning. Lefors said, "I don't let go, friend Tom. I've nearly had 'em a couple times, and I've lost 'em, I'll allow that. But they're goin' no place I won't follow them, you can lay your money on that. I go after a man, that man's as good as got, one way or another, one year or another."

Horn nodded again, pulled the cork from a fresh bottle of whiskey, and slopped some into his glass. His head seemed to be floating a little way above his body, bobbing lightly in the air like that balloon the dumb Signal Corps had hoisted at the approach to San Juan Hill. Drew a lot of Spanish fire right on Pershing's black troops and Roosevelt's Rough Riders until the Spaniards brought it down; but it had looked pretty and carefree up there. When a man's head felt like that, he could cut loose and say what he wanted to, devil take his hindquarters, or whatever the hell the saying was, and needlepoint around with the facts until hell wouldn't have it.

"Now, friend Joe," he said, "we talking about man-hunting, I'll tell you somming about manhunting."

Lefors looked toward the just-ajar door.

Smalley held the pistol tight with both hands, but it wavered, the sight drifting from Horn's forehead to his nose to his chin. The sheriff gritted his teeth and reluctantly loosened one hand from the butt, reaching it down to prod the sleeping man with an extended forefinger.

There was no response; the whiskey fumes arising from the sleeper told him why. Smalley poked Horn again. "Mr. Horn? Mr. Horn, please?"

Horn mumbled, "Oh, hey, Eddie," and rolled over in his bed.

Smalley prodded him once more, urgently. "You got to get up, and that's no fooling."

"Christ-o-mighty, why?" Horn said faintly, his eyes still closed.

" 'Cause I've got to arrest you."

Horn blinked up at the sheriff, taking in the wavering gun and the worried face. None of it made any sense; but then, he was too hung over for anything to make sense. Best go along with what was happening and try to sort it out afterwards. He reached down and grabbed a boot. He hoped it was the left one, since his left foot was on that side of the bed, and he wasn't sure he could work out just now how to get his right foot over to where the boot was.

* * *

A bald deputy with something withdrawn in his look let Noble into Horn's cell. Horn sat on his cot, braiding lengths of cord; it seemed to him, as he looked up, that Noble was damned mad about something.

Noble sat beside him and opened the leather portfolio he was carrying. "They're actually going to try you for the murder of that boy," he said. He removed a long yellow pad of paper crossed with blue lines from the portfolio. "Tom, you don't have to take me to be your lawyer, I may not be the best, but no one charges more and gets away with it, so I guess that means something."

Horn, his fingers still working, said tiredly, "You're my man, Mr. Noble." He glanced at the man next to him. "What makes 'em think I did it?"

"They're being very damn mysterious," Noble said heavily. "Big surprise, they say." He took a pen from his vest, and a flat pocket inkwell and flipped its lid open. "You got any character witnesses you want to use? I'll bring 'em in from anywhere, money don't matter to me here, they got me mad."

Horn considered. Old Geronimo, he'd have as much about his character to say as anybody, but he didn't see the old Apache—old as God, now, he must be, but still hanging on, down there in Florida—cutting much ice in a Cheyenne courtroom. And there wouldn't, probably, be anything to interpret for him except Horn himself, which he didn't see the judge taking kindly to. "Could you get Al Sieber up from Arizona? Most likely Globe or Tucson."

Noble nodded and sent his pen scratching across

the pad. "Mr. Noble?" The cattleman-lawyer looked up.

"What *kind* of a surprise?"

The courtroom, Horn saw, was jammed. He had expected that; when they'd brought him here from the jail this morning, there had been a line stretching out to the street and around the corner: men, women, children, lots of them carrying lunches. I never drew a crowd like this at the Phoenix Fair, time I won that damn medal, he thought.

He assessed the judge and the jury. They looked okay, no obvious drunks, nut cases, or dummies among them. There would be a lot of hot air floating around, but with something this dumb, no problem about how it'd turn out. He was glad he had been firm with Ernestina about staying away. Since there was no real case here, the prosecution would probably bring up a lot of stuff that he'd rather tell her in his own time, if ever.

"Big turnout," he muttered to Noble, who sat next to him, shuffling a sheaf of notes.

"Everybody wants to see the notorious Tom Horn," Noble whispered. "Hoping to hear you sentenced to hang, though that's not about to happen."

Horn was puzzled. Why would anybody feel that way about him?

". . . I tried getting to my boy, but they shot at me. Ten, *fifteen* times, they shot at me," Kel Nickell said from the witness stand.

". . . and when we got to him," Mrs. Nickell, drawn

and old-looking, said, "Willie was *dead,* shot dead . . . and someone had put a rock under his head and . . ."

"That *proves* someone's tryin' to put it on me," Horn said urgently. "Rocks and that, anyone could find them and use them. I ever backshot somebody, let alone a kid, I wouldn't for damn sure of advertised it, for chrissakes."

Noble pursed his lips and jotted on the pad in front of him.

". . . and as well as acting deputy, you are also a qualified stenographer, is that correct, Mr. Snow?" the prosecuting attorney said.

The bald man who had acted as Horn's turnkey in jail said, "Yessir."

"And the transcript we are about to hear, it is verbatim?"

"Yessir. Every word, verbatim," Snow said earnestly.

"What transcript of *what?*" Horn whispered to Noble. Noble shook his head. "Must be that big surprise you was talking of," Horn muttered.

The prosecutor looked toward the back of the courtroom and said, more loudly than he had been speaking, aware of the dramatic quality of what he had to say, "Joe Lefors to the stand!"

"Well, hell, they got their wires crossed this time," Horn whispered to Noble. "They put old Joe on, he'll set 'em straight about me, blow the whole damn . . ." He fell silent as he saw Lefors walking down the aisle of the courtroom, grim-faced and carrying a sheaf of papers.

* * *

". . . most of the day before I hit Cheyenne I spend out at the Nickell place, studying the murder site. Soon as I saw the spot and heard about the rock, well, it wasn't much of a problem figuring who did it; no, the problem was making him come clean."

Lefors looked at the prosecutor and the jury; somehow he did not happen to look in Horn's direction. "Late that afternoon, I met Horn and challenged him to a little drinking bout—he drinks heavy, always has—and I took a suite at the Inter Ocean and stationed Deputy Snow in the next room, close enough so he could get all that was spoke."

"Did you drink with him?" Noble whispered to Horn. Horn nodded. "Was the connecting door open?"

Horn tried to recall the scene. "Might of been."

"Deputy Snow put everything down *just as it was spoken?*" the prosecutor asked. Lefors nodded. "For the record, please answer yes or no, Marshal Lefors."

"Yes."

"And that is the transcript you now hold in your hand?"

"It is." Lefors opened the sheaf of papers and, for the first time, looked at Horn. Their eyes met and held. Lefors would have given much to be able to look away, but he could not; the icy blue of Horn's eyes held him as though mesmerized. What he read there of himself and of the man whose gaze he could not evade, no one ever knew, not even Lefors himself; but he slumped in relief when, after close to a minute, the prosecutor moved between them and cut the almost visible connection that riveted them together.

"Go on, please, Mr. Lefors," the prosecutor said.

Lefors settled himself into the witness chair, held

the sheaf of papers almost at arm's length, squinted at them, and said, "This is a true and complete account of the conversation between myself and Thomas Horn on the evening of April twelfth, nineteen hundred and one. 'Horn: You have a good lash-up here, and I see there is plenty of the good stuff ready.'"

Horn stirred in his seat. Noble leaned to him and asked, "That what you said?"

"Amounted to that," Horn said. "Don't sound much like me, does it, though?"

"'Lefors: I studied where the Nickell boy was killed, and if you was waiting long, you must have got awful hungry.'

"'Horn: Friend Joe, sometimes I get so hungry I would kill my mother for some grub, but I never quit until I get my man.'"

The courtroom was deathly still. Horn stared, wide-eyed, at Lefors. "It's all *somethin'* like what I said, but not *what* I said," he whispered to Noble.

"'Lefors: How much do you get per killing? Friend Joe—' sorry, this is Horn now," Lefors said, looking up from the papers at the prosecutor. "'Friend Joe, it all depends on how fat are my employers, but I would say that six hundred dollars a piece is a fair average.'"

Horn gave Noble a glance, and muttered, "Was I bragging on that, I'd of gone up, not down."

"'Lefors: Why did you put the rock under the kid's head after he was dead?'

"'Horn: That is the way I hang out my sign to collect money for this kind of a job.'

"'Lefors: Does it ever get to bothering you?'

"'Horn: Whyever should it get to bothering me, Friend Joe? Killing is my specialty. I look on it as a

216

business proposition and I think I have a corner on the market.'"

Horn snatched Noble's yellow pad and scribbled on it with a pencil; the point tore into the paper. LIES LIES LIES!

Lefors took a deep breath. The papers rattled in his hands as he looked away from them, then at them again. "'Lefors: How far was Willie Nickell when you killed him?'

"'Horn: About three hundred yards. It was the best shot I ever made and the dirtiest trick I ever done—'"

A wordless shout came from a man at the rear of the courtroom; then men and women were standing and crying out; some reached for Horn and were driven back by Noble and a bailiff, who did not seem to have his heart in his work.

The judge hammered his gavel steadily, but the chaos continued. After a few moments of uproar, he bawled, "Court's adjourned for the day! Bailiff, take the prisoner back to his cell!"

The last thing Horn saw as he was hustled from the courtroom was a sea of hate-filled faces.

CHAPTER 23

Horn stood unmoving, looking out the window of his cell. It gave him a view of the packed earth of the courtyard and the outer wall of the jail. Small openings in the wall showed details of buildings outside, but not enough for him to identify any one of them. He tried to remember what might be across the street from the jail; but it was not a neighborhood he had been in the habit of visiting. A peeling green corner of a roof might have belonged to a bar he'd been in once, he thought, but there was no way of being sure.

His hands held a length of partly braided rope, but were still.

A clatter of feet and a protesting voice came to him from the corridor, and he slowly turned toward the barred door. "Mrs. Irwin," Sheriff Smalley said plaintively, "you're not his lawyer—that's the only visitor he's supposed to have."

"Oh, Ed, stop it." Horn stirred as if reluctantly coming alive, when he heard her voice.

"I'll let you talk to him through the bars, all right?"

"No it isn't all right. *I want to see Tom.*"

Then they were outside the door, Smalley looking

angry and worried and fussy, Ernestina calmly determined.

"Just don't *tell* nobody," Smalley said. He unlocked the door and opened it; Ernestina stepped inside. Smalley relocked the door, moved to the far side of the corridor and leaned against it, arms folded.

"Ed, will you just *move*?" she said. "I haven't got a gun in my purse, I promise." Smalley gave an aggrieved sigh and stamped away. She turned to Horn and whispered, "But I do have a file."

Horn looked at her blankly. "A file?"

Ernestina nodded. "For the bars." She nodded toward the window.

Horn gave her a long, level look. His lips twitched, and he threw back his head and laughed—not in mockery but in genuine hilarity. "Ernestina," he said, when the spasm had subsided, "that's just the *sweetest* thought . . ."

He reached for her and drew her close to him.

". . . but I think you're supposed to bring them in a cake, that's the regular way."

She pushed against his chest, freeing herself from his embrace, and said hotly, "It isn't funny! You're being railroaded, don't you know that? Before you cleaned out Brown's Hole rustling *was* the biggest business around, and all that kind, they want you dead so they can go back into operation! And all the Wyoming Cattle Club—not Noble but all those senators and governors—they've got to be scared to death you'll tell they hired you, so they want you gone, too." She put her hands on his shoulders and looked into his face; her lips were trembling and her eyes half closed, as if she could not bear to see him too clearly. "I'm all there is on your side, Tom."

"Then I can't lose, can I, Ernestina?" Horn said softly. He reached up and laid his hands on hers where they rested on his shoulders, then slowly slid them down her arms, brushing the fabric of her dress gently, sliding over her shoulders and drawing her to him.

She let herself go limp in his arms, feeling his warmth and maleness against her, shutting out all other thought and feeling . . . except for the hateful, cold fragment of her mind that was carefully memorizing every sensation, down to the harsh scent of him and the roughness of his shirt against her cheek, as though the memories would be all she would ever have.

The haggard old derelict slumped in the witness chair, his gnarled hands clutching two canes, and looked blearily around the courtroom. The prosecutor glanced at the jury and took in their expressions with satisfaction. No cross-examination needed for this one; he'd do the defense enough harm just by being what he obviously was.

Horn felt dead inside. What was happening to him was bad, but it was at least happening to someone who was near enough what Tom Horn had been once so that it somehow mattered; a kind of dying a man could live with, so to speak. But what could happen when you went on living after everything had gone, that was worse.

"I knew him years," Al Sieber said. "And never once did a curse word come from him . . . never once would he *touch* whiskey . . . ." Noble, sitting next to Horn, sighed and rested his forehead in one hand. "Never *once* . . . ." Sieber smiled weakly at the stony-faced jury.

"He saved me from Apache ambush and he brought Crawford back even though he was wounded"—Sieber touched his right arm—"here, shot here, bad and bleeding, but he brought back Crawford and . . ." He looked again at the jury and seemed to shrink back in the chair.

Horn caught Sieber's eye and smiled and nodded encouragingly to him.

Sieber sat huddled for a long moment, like nothing so much as a straw-stuffed scarecrow flung into a chair, except that his lips worked silently as he tried to puzzle out what to say next.

He gave a deep, shuddering sigh and hauled himself upright on his canes. When he spoke again, his voice was firmer and deeper. "I tell you something . . . I tell you all something." He stopped and looked down. "No, I don't mean that. I mean I *ask* you all something." He nodded toward where Lefors sat in the front rank of spectators. "Lefors, you I understand . . ."

Lefors' face tightened; his fingers, spread on the flat straw hat in his lap, tensed.

"Once you was something, now you're a bum like me, you make up confessions for rewards, how much for this one, three thousand dollars?" Sieber was swaying, clutching the canes with twisted, white-knuckled hands. "I knew many men, great men, men you never *heard* of in this room . . . ." His puffy eyes seemed to sharpen as he looked over the heads of the crowd and through the windows to the vacancy of sky beyond, and his voice came like a roll of war drums now: "*Taza* and *Loco* and *Mangas* Coloradas, and some you heard of . . . Cochise and Geronimo, and we brought them all down, and not one of them could do what Horn could do, and that's what I got to ask you . . ." His voice faltered once more, and he blinked rapidly. "What law says we got to do it. . . ?" He shook his head, subsiding again into the walking ragbag he had been at the start of his testimony, looking at the floor and mumbling, "Why do we bring them down?"

"Yes, I was drinking, sure I was drunk," Horn said impatiently. "Give me enough whiskey, I'd probably tell you I shot Jesus if that's what you wanted to hear—but I don't talk the way that confession has me sounding and everybody who knows me knows that's true. What was it, 'It all depends on how fat are my employers'?—I can't hardly get my tongue around that one, and I don't think a man of you could, either."

The jury, Horn saw, at least looked as if it was paying attention to him. He thought he saw two of the jurymen's lips move as if they were trying out the sentence silently. He leaned forward in the witness chair and spoke directly to them. "I don't know about most of you, but when I'm drinking hard, I don't recall too much the next morning, but I do remember him asking me was the rock a sign and I said I supposed it was. *But I never said I put it there.* I *didn't* put it there. Why would I ambush a baby, shoot him in the back? Ask the Army, ask the Pinkertons, ask anybody you want, 'Would Tom Horn do a thing like that?' No, Christ-o-mighty, no, *never*."

He sat back in the chair and looked around at the spectators, then back at the jury. He said, softly and earnestly, "I didn't do it."

He waited for a question from Noble, from the prosecutor, for some reaction from the crowd or the jury; there was none. "What can I tell you, I didn't do it . . . ." He looked once more around the silent courtroom and found himself giving an unintended quick nervous smile as he repeated, "I didn't . . . ."

"If the jury's out for more than two hours, we're home free," Noble said in an undertone. "They talk it over that long, they're not going to work themselves up to hang you, the ones for hanging talk themselves out of their righteous fury."

"They been out how long now?" Horn said.

"Twenty minutes."

Horn cocked his head to one side. It seemed he could hear footsteps in the corridor behind the courtroom. The doors opened, and the bailiff approached the bench and muttered in the judge's ear. The bailiff vanished through the door, and reappeared in a moment, leading the twelve jurymen, each of whom found some part of the floor or wall a great deal more interesting to look at than Horn.

CHAPTER 24

Horn lay on his cot, braiding. Not a *riata* this time; he didn't know anyone who would be able to make any better use of the kind he could turn out than of an ordinary one, so there would be no sense of it. His fingers twisted long strands of horsehair, forming a bridle. There would be some use for that, and it would look mighty elegant.

The gloom in the cell, caused by the square of canvas fastened over the window, made it difficult to see the horsehair, but his fingers did the work almost automatically.

Outside, he heard a heavy thump, then Ed Smalley's low voice: "Now, dammit, why didn't that work?"

Another voice replied, "Patience. Mine is the best gallows, but nothing worthwhile is ever easy."

"Well, fix it," Smalley said angrily.

Horn stood and went to the window. "Troubles, Eddie?"

"Sorry, Tom."

"How long I got?" Horn asked.

"Sixteen hours more."

Horn called, "Pull the canvas off?"

After a moment, Smalley said, "You sure?"

"It's worse not seeing it," Horn said.

He heard Smalley call an order. The canvas jerked, then dropped away. He could see the courtyard and the mechanism that stood in it. The top part of it was plain enough: a heavy upright and crosspiece standing on a platform. The noose wasn't in place yet, but it was clearly a gallows. The platform was raised about eight feet from the earth, and beneath it was a jumble of pulleys and a long trough, with two fat metal containers, about five feet high, at either end. One of Smalley's deputies was pumping water from a large barrel into one of the containers, while the sheriff and a small man in a rumpled suit—the inventor, he supposed—stood and looked on impatiently. Horn studied the apparatus. Looked like it worked with counterweights: one drum was filled with enough water to outweigh the man on the platform and hold the trap door in place; then a cock was opened and water ran along the trough to the other drum, and when the man outweighed the water that was left, the trap opened. It reminded him of a patent reaper he'd seen once, over in Nebraska—that had done the job well enough, but was so complicated and full of parts that kept breaking down or having to be adjusted that two men with scythes could get the same amount of wheat in. Given time, Horn was sure he could work out something that would work a lot better and be a lot simpler.

He went back to the cot, lay down, and began braiding again. Some people, most people, make too much of a fuss about everything, he thought, gussy it up with machines and what-all and fancy plans. Nelson A. Miles and his heliograph, for instance, when what it came down to, what it had been all along, was that someone who knew how had to go after Geronimo and bring him back. And in Cuba, everybody running around and jumping up and down over what to do about the mules when the transports couldn't get in close to the beach—how come it had to be me that saw what to do was push 'em over the side and swim 'em ashore?

Geronimo, now . . . he didn't bother puzzling out all the time should he do this or should he do that or wouldn't the other maybe be better? When it come to him that he had to make war, he made war; and when he knew he was licked, he gave in. Of course, there's Geronimo, still steaming away down in Florida, and here's me, where I am. It don't seem as though the fancy folks can stand to have the ones like us around, like old Al said.

He wondered briefly why that should be, but gave it up. What mattered was not why something happened, but that it happened . . .

A key rattled in the door. Deputy Snow fumbled at the lock, a tray of food balanced on one hand.

. . . or what could be made to happen.

Snow kept one hand on his gun butt as he bent to set the tray on the small table. His hand had hardly time to clench on it when Horn seemed to flow from his stretched-out position on the cot, slam into him, and smash him against the cell wall.

Horn snatched Snow's gun and keys, chopped at his head once with the pistol barrel, and ran from the cell, leaving the deputy unconscious on the floor. He grinned as he pounded through the corridor, through the jail offices, where only a startled clerk on lunch-time duty looked up, open-mouthed, as he passed, and down the front steps of the building into the open air.

An old woman at the foot of the stairs saw him, recognized him, saw the gun he held, and screamed. A couple walking a few feet behind her took up the cry. Horn ran toward the nearest alley.

In the jail courtyard, Sheriff Smalley, eating his lunch, lifted his head as the yelling came to him, said, "Jesus!" and ran for the door that led to the jail.

When Smalley got into the street, it was in a turmoil, with people pouring out of buildings, yelling to each other that Horn was out and armed, to go after him, to get back inside—everything, Smalley thought bitterly, except where the sonofabitch had *gone*. The bell in a nearby church began to ring; then another.

In the street ahead of him, a small boy looked up, pointed, and jumped happily up and down. Smalley and the crowd around him looked in the same direction and saw Horn running along a rooftop. Smalley and several men near him pounded along the street in the same direction; Smalley noted dryly that he seemed to be able to outdistance the others pretty easily.

Knots of people ahead pointed and yelled. He could catch lightning-quick glimpses of Horn jumping from a roof to a porch, to the next roof, then dropping over the edge of one building and out of sight.

Smalley rounded the corner of an alley that ended in a high fence in time to see Horn clearing it. Smalley ran at it and jumped; one foot caught on the top and he slammed into the ground on the other side. He scrambled to his feet and looked around dazedly, panting hard. The street ahead was empty, no clue to which way Horn had gone. But the building on the right was a stable. Odds were, Horn would be there, saddling up and getting ready to ride. There was a side door to the stable near him; he cocked his revolver and eased the door open, guarding against any warning creak of the hinges. He stepped through the doorway silently, seeing only the dim shapes of the patiently standing horses, hearing only the light stamping one of them made. Maybe Horn was blocks away, still running, and—

"Wrong door, Eddie," Horn's voice came from behind him. Smalley froze. Horn's hand snaked around him and gently plucked the gun from his grasp. "Walk forward."

Smalley took a step and said, "What happens now?"

"I don't much want to hurt you," Horn said quietly.

"You're gonna have to," Smalley said. "Look out that window." He pointed toward the window facing the main street. It was dusty and cobwebbed, filming the glare of the early afternoon, but Horn could see that the street was packed with people, fifty at least, men, women, and children.

Horn's face was expressionless as he turned away and made final adjustments to the gear of the horse he had been saddling.

"You're gonna have to kill me and a dozen more to make it past," Smalley went on. "You've got two guns, if anyone can do it, you can, but even with a dozen dead, there's still gonna be millions of us and one of you."

Horn's eyes closed briefly, and a quick flash of a

natural bowl in the rock and two men hunkered around a small fire came to him.

"Maybe you can make it to the mountains—you're murder in the mountains—but you gotta come down sometime. And when you do there's still gonna be millions of us waiting. And only one of you."

"Open the main door, Eddie," Horn said in a low voice.

"Open it yourself."

"I never yet killed an innocent man." Horn's tone was almost pleading.

"You're gonna have to kill a *bunch* if I open that door, so you might as well get used to it." He turned to face Horn, stared at him defiantly, and said, "Shoot." He could see in the gloom of the stable that the gun was trained on his chest. "I got no family, you took Ernestina, there's no one gonna mourn me, you couldn't ask for a better man to start on. There's still gonna be millions of us and only one of you."

Horn looked at him almost absently. Then he reached to where his lariat hung from the flanks of the horse and took it down. Smalley could not move, and found that he was breathing shallowly as he watched Horn gently open the coil of supple rope and set it spinning. It whispered from the hay-strewn stable floor and seemed to float up his body, moving close to and away from him like a living circle. It rose above his head, then settled almost to the floor; Smalley could not follow the swift motions of arm and hand that kept it whirling. Horn leaped lightly into the spinning circle of rope and out, following its motion, dancing with it.

He seemed so eerily intent on what he was doing

that it came as a shock to Smalley when he spoke. "I was real handy with these once." He continued the intricate dance with the rope. "I remember, I tried showing off for Ernestina." The rope rose and fell about him. "Those were the good days."

The spinning rope rose shoulder-high. Above it, Horn shook his head. "No, they weren't." The rope dropped to the floor and lay limply about him.

Smalley opened the door to Horn's cell. As they stood before it, he said to Horn, "You never killed that kid, did you?"

Horn looked at him but said nothing.

"Then why'd you surrender just now?"

Horn turned and silently walked into the cell.

"Then what the hell did you *escape* for?"

Horn sat on the cot and looked up at him. After a while, he said, " 'Cause I could."

The bridle was almost done. It would be a good one, but Horn had expected that. Once you learned how to work with anything, horsehair, cord, trail sign, there was no trick to keep on doing it right, no reason to do it any other way.

Sieber, seated outside in the corridor, passed the whiskey bottle through the bars under the watchful eyes of Ed Smalley, who stood, pistol out and ready, a little distance away.

Horn took a long drink and looked at Sieber. "You drink a better brand of whiskey when you visit me in jail."

"Probably just tastes better," Sieber said.

Horn thought that over for a while, then nodded.

He said gravely, trying for Sieber's slightly guttural tone, "It is so."

Sieber smiled. Horn drank again, then passed the bottle to him. He shook his head. "I don't hold it as good as I used to."

"You never held it good," Horn said mockingly.

Sieber looked pleased. "I didn't?" He reached for the bottle. "Then why not?" He tilted the bottle up. Horn's fingers resumed their work. He exhaled noisily after the drink and said, "Remember Micky Free?"

"The little Apache who thought he couldn't get killed?"

Sieber nodded and handed the bottle back through the bars. "I heard from him."

"Didn't know he could write," Horn said, and took another drink.

"Well, it was mostly pictures."

Horn looked at Sieber. "Can you write?"

Sieber's brow furrowed, and he squinted at Horn. "I can make all the numbers," he said finally.

Horn grinned. "That's half the battle."

From down the corridor, Smalley could see, far into the night, the bottle passing back and forth between the man in the cell and the man in the corridor.

They began gathering by dawn.

Families, couples, people on their own; most dressed in Sunday best as if going to hear a president or a preacher deliver an address; some with picnic baskets packed with the breakfast they had skipped at home in order to get in place early.

The choicest spots were those opposite the high, narrow windows in the wall of the jail's courtyard.

Nothing but the wall of the jail building itself could be seen through them, but the view seemed to bring the lucky spectators a touch closer to the proceedings inside. A line of uniformed militiamen stood along the base of the wall, keeping the crowd from approaching it closely. One enterprising boy shimmied up a tall tree and found a perch that commanded a partial view of the courtyard.

There was nothing to do now but wait. It would not be long.

The canvas had been replaced over the window in the cell, but Horn did not need more light to put the finishing touches to the horsehair bridle. He sat working on it, dressed in a soft shirt, open at the throat, and dark trousers, for a moment, then rose and handed it to Smalley.

The sheriff, dressed in a dark jacket, with a stiff white collar and string tie chafing his neck, looked miserable and nervous. He fumbled with the bridle for a moment, then stuffed it in his pocket.

Horn took the first step out of the cell; Smalley nearly stumbled as he hurried to keep pace with him. At the door leading to the courtyard, Horn stopped and looked down.

The enclosure was thronged; there was not a clear foot of space, except where the gallows stood. "Who are they?" Horn asked.

"Newspapermen, a bunch of sheriffs and marshals, some doctors, a whole bunch of visiting dignitaries," Smalley muttered. Horn nodded, and the two men started down the stone steps leading to the yard.

Horn heard a single shrill yell from outside, then a murmur that built to a screaming roar.

The boy in the tree yelled, "They're bringing him in—Horn's being drug down!" Beneath him, the crowd stirred, then began to call out and yell frenziedly.

"What's happening now?" a grizzled man bawled up to him.

The teen-ager shook his head. The figure in the open-necked shirt was hidden in the sea of people inside the courtyard.

Sieber stood at the bottom of the steps leading up to the gallows platform, holding himself erect with a tight grip on his canes. As Horn approached, he said softly, "Can I do anything?"

Horn's lips quirked in a near smile; he shook his head and walked a step past Sieber. He stopped and turned. "Yeah."

"What?"

"Sing 'Life's Stairway to Heaven.'"

"I can't sing," Sieber said. "I sing *horrible*."

Horn turned away and mounted the first step. "Right, right."

He was at the third step when Sieber's cracked, off-key voice began the hymn: "'Life is like a mountain railroad . . .'"

Horn shook his head very slightly. Sieber was telling the truth about that, all right. Horrible was pretty close to it.

"'With an engineer that's brave,
"'We must make the run successful,
"'From the cradle to the grave.'"

They were on the platform now. Smalley struggled with the stiff, new harness that would pinion Horn's arms and legs. Horn stood quietly. Smalley was sweating and mumbling, jabbing a recalcitrant strap into a buckle that refused to receive it.

> " 'Watch the curves, the fills, the tunnels;
> " 'Never falter, never quail;
> " 'Keep your hand upon the throttle
> " 'And your eye upon the rail.' "

The boy in the tree had a better view, now that the principals in the scene were on the main stage of the drama. "They're trussing him good!" he yelled.

"Is the bastard frightened?" the grizzled man on the ground called.

"He's shaking like a sonofabitch!"

The volume of the crowd's roaring rose yet higher.

Looking back, Joe Lefors could see the straggle of buildings that marked the edge of Cheyenne and, farther off, the cluster of taller, solider buildings in the center of town. He did not think the jail was visible from where he was. His face was tight, closed, the eyes shadowed by the brim of his straw skimmer.

He had been riding slowly, at a comfortable pace for himself and his mount; but now he turned, jabbed his heels into the horse's side, and leaned forward. It seemed to him for some reason that he had to ride very fast, for a long time.

The thick walls and double-glazed windows of the Wyoming Cattle Club kept most of the noise of the street crowd out, but some filtered through. The twelve members could see the surging throng—pushing past each other, some jumping up for an instant's better view, some hawking souvenirs of the great day—but not the jail.

There was a subdued cheerfulness, an air of a burden lifted, about the twelve men. John Noble smiled broadly.

"We are *all* young la*dies* . . ."

Mandy Irwin skipped rope in time to the chant, intent on keeping the rope moving at just the right speed, slapping the ground just ahead of her shoes as she lifted them.

". . . and *we* are *sure* to *die.*"

Ernestina watched her from the porch of the hotel. There was no one else in the street. She stared at her daughter, willing herself not to hear the distant sound of exultant voices.

Horn was now almost completely strapped into the harness, in spite of Smalley's nervous clumsiness. There was a final strap that was giving Smalley more trouble than any of the others. Horn looked down at him and said, "I'm the one dying—keep your nerve."

Smalley took a deep breath. "Yessir." The strap slid into place and was caught by the buckle tongue. He moved Horn to the center of the platform, picked up the noose, and held it ready to place around Horn's neck. "Any last words, Tom?"

Horn looked around, taking in the lawmen, the newspaper reporters scratching away on their pads, the important-looking men who had to be politicians of some kind—no Wyoming Cattle Club members; there wouldn't be, he thought, would there?—and then the window in the courtyard wall through which the screaming of the mob outside came.

"Anything at all?" Smalley said.

The straps were too tight around Horn for him to shrug. "You can't hurt a Christian."

Smalley reached up to adjust the noose.

Sieber was rock-steady on his canes, and his voice was stronger, though no more harmonious:

> "'As you roll across the trestle,
> "'Spanning Jordan's swelling tide,
> "'You behold the Union Depot
> "'Into which the train will glide.'"

Smalley stepped back and pushed a lever. Under the roar from outside and Sieber's singing a new sound came as water began to drain from the counter-weight drum.

> "'There you'll meet the Superintendent,
> "'God the Father, God the Son,
> "'With the hearty, joyous plaudit,
> "'"Weary Pilgrim, Welcome Home."
> "'Put your trust alone in Jesus—'"

At the sound of the slam of the trap opening and the heavy thump that followed, Sieber stopped singing.

A young boy in the Catskills develops into a famous and breathtakingly skillful magician— with something to hide. His attempt to keep his secret from the public draws him onto a bizarre course that subtly leads into thrilling and psychologically terrifying regions.

MAGIC

A dazzling psychological thriller
by **William Goldman**
author of *Marathon Man*

"Eerie . . . psychic . . . startling. The goose bumps grow a little further in your arms as predictable events somehow become unpredictable."
—*Chicago Book World*

"This dazzling psychological thriller cannot be put down." —*St. Louis Post-Dispatch*

"A brilliantly alarming novel." —*Cosmopolitan*

A DELL BOOK $1.95

DELL'S ACTION-PACKED WESTERNS

Selected Titles

At your local bookstore or use this handy coupon for ordering: